Praise for
Eavesdropping on Lucifer

"*Eavesdropping on Lucifer* is common sense, digestible wisdom that can be easily understood by every generation. C.S. Lewis would have given it his stamp of approval."
–The Honorable John Ashcroft
Former U.S. Attorney General

"My advocacy work is to build a culture of life, defend the institution of marriage, and to protect religious freedom. *Eavesdropping on Lucifer* is an easy to read, fascinating explanation of the forces of evil that we need to overcome to ensure families thrive, life is cherished and religious freedom flourishes."
–Karen Bowling
Executive Director, Nebraska Family Alliance

"This is an interesting book written by an interesting man. One does not usually associate Harvard-educated public servants with a book addressing biblical themes. We should be glad that Don is unusual in this way, for he reminds us of something the Bible asserts from beginning to end: there is an unseen spiritual reality that affects the world in which we live."

–Kyle McClellan
Pastor, Grace Church PCA
Author of *Mea Culpa: Learning From Mistakes in Ministry*

"Donald B. Stenberg provides a different approach to assessing evil in the modern world that, like C.S. Lewis' *The Screwtape Letters*, is all the more accessible to ordinary readers because of its fictional, conversation-based overlay. Christians who want an accessible, chatty blend of pointed observation, reflective insights, and fun will find *Eavesdropping on Lucifer* excels in the kinds of insights and lessons that keep readers engaged, thinking, and entertained, all in one.

–D. Donovan
Senior Reviewer, Midwest Book Review

Eavesdropping
on Lucifer

Donald B. Stenberg

Carpenter's Son Publishing

Published by Carpenter's Son Publishing, Franklin, Tennessee

Published in association with Larry Carpenter of
Christian Book Services, LLC
www.christianbookservices.com

Cover Design by Adept Content Solutions

Interior Design by Suzanne Lawing

Edited by Adept Content Solutions

Printed in the United States of America

978-1-949572-88-9

You look like an angel
Walk like an angel
Talk like an angel
But I got wise
You're the devil in disguise

FROM A SONG BY ELVIS PRESLEY

Preface

Having spent half of my adult life in public office and half as a practicing lawyer, writing a fictional book about the devil and his evil work is not something that I ever planned to do—or even thought of doing. I have no formal training as a theologian.

But the words of the book flowed into my mind somehow, and I wrote them down. True, I had to do some research on the details of history and science that you will come across as you read the book. But the basic idea for use of those facts simply came to me.

The history of the support for religion by the government and the courts in the United States will surprise some who are not familiar with it. In the book *Lucifer*, "the Boss" explains how that dramatically changed. Likewise, some of the scientific evidence of creation and the flood will come as a surprise to many, because the media chooses not to tell that story.

The book begins with a meeting between the Boss and Jonathan, his would-be apprentice. The Boss explains to Jonathan the tools he has used to corrupt modern-day culture.

When the Boss sends Jonathan out to put those tools into practice, he encounters Angelica, who has been sent to do good and oppose evil. There is an underlying theme of salvation through the Son of God.

The book is easy to read, entertaining, and thought-provoking. I hope that you will enjoy it and take away a deeper understanding of good and evil.

DONALD B. STENBERG

About the Author

Donald B. Stenberg has an undergraduate degree in physics with minors in chemistry and mathematics from the University of Nebraska–Lincoln where he was inducted into the national scholastic honorary Phi Beta Kappa. He received a juris doctorate degree with honors from Harvard Law School and a master's degree in business administration from Harvard Business School.

In addition to his private law practice, Mr. Stenberg was elected to and served three terms as Nebraska's Attorney General and two terms as Nebraska's State Treasurer. He has argued several cases in the Supreme Court of the United States, including the *Stenberg v. Carhart* case, in which he defended Nebraska's law banning partial-birth abortion.

Contents

Chapter 1

)) There Is No Devil

Jonathan knocked nervously on the Boss's door.

"Come in. Come in."

Jonathan entered the Boss's study with a mixture of anticipation and fear. The Boss waved him into a chair and continued writing on a pad on his desk.

Jonathan took the opportunity to look around the Boss's study. He had never been here before but had heard some of the stories from those who had.

Just as he had been told, the study was full of a collection of antiquities—a replica of a golden calf, a bronze statue of Molech, tools from a medieval torture chamber, the sword used to execute John the Baptist, a charred post used in the execution of Joan of Arc, and many other items Jonathan couldn't identify. Jonathan's gaze swept back to the Boss, and he looked at him carefully as the Boss continued to write.

He was a handsome man with dark black hair, square

chin and a high forehead. His appearance was that of a man of about fifty years old, slim, in good health, and apparently excellent physical condition. *Dressed in a suit and tie, he could have easily passed for a banker, a lawyer, a business-man, or even a man of the cloth,* Jonathan thought.

Just then, the Boss looked up at Jonathan and stared at him intently.

"I understand that you graduated at the top of your class at the Academy, Jonathan."

"Yes, sir," said Jonathan, beaming with pride.

"Do you know why you are here?" asked the Boss.

"Not exactly, sir."

"Well, I am in need of a new apprentice. I have heard good reports about you, and I wanted to see if you might be the right person for the job. To start with, I have a few questions for you."

"Yes, sir," said Jonathan excitedly.

"Tell me, then, what do we want people to think the devil looks like," asked the Boss with a pleasant smile.

"Well, sir, at the Academy we were taught that we should treat that as a silly question. It is a silly question because the devil does not exist. No intelligent, rational person can possibly believe such a fairy tale. It is nothing but an old superstition. It came from the imagination of uneducated men who lived centuries ago. In those days parents would keep their children in line by telling them that if they didn't obey their parents the devil would—"

"Yes, excellent answer," said the Boss.

"And why do we want people to believe that the devil

does not exist?" asked the Boss.

"Because if they don't believe there is a devil, it will be easier to lead them into our way of thinking. Their guard will be down," Jonathan said, just as he had been taught at the Academy.

"Correct," said the Boss.

"Sir, may I ask you a question?"

"Certainly," smiled the Boss.

"Where did the idea come from that the devil is all red and has horns and a pointed tail and a pitchfork?" Jonathan asked.

"That's a great question," the Boss said, laughing. "Several millennia ago I did make a few appearances looking just as you described. The reason I did it is this: while our primary objective is to convince people that there is no devil, there will always be some doubters. Some people who think that maybe there is a devil.

"For them, we want them to think the devil is all red and has horns and all the rest. Then when they are talking to a handsome, friendly man or a beautiful, sensual woman the idea that they are talking to the devil will never enter their minds.

"Let's face it, Jonathan. If a human met someone with horns and a long tail and all that, they would be scared to death. There is no way we could be effective looking like that. They would run away. They wouldn't believe a word we said."

"I get it, Boss," Jonathan said. "Sir, at the Academy we studied how successful you have been at convincing people that there is no such thing as the devil."

"Yes, it's one of my greatest accomplishments. And it has not been easy to convince people of that while at the same time encouraging and facilitating war, murder, abortion, adultery, robberies, drug overdoses, and all the rest."

"Yes, sir. At the Academy we studied your methods of convincing people that there is no devil," Jonathan said proudly.

"I'm glad you brought that up. Tell me what you were taught," the Boss replied.

"We were taught that the most powerful tool we have for this purpose is ridicule. And if that doesn't work in a particular case, then we appeal to reason and logic."

"Can you give me a specific example of the use of these tools from your in-service training?" asked the Boss.

"Yes, sir. I was on a college campus as a student. One night several of us were talking, and one guy said his parents warned him not to let the devil tempt him into evil things at college like drug use, or cheating on exams, or premarital sex.

"So, I immediately put my training into practice. I started by laughing at him, and several of the other students joined in. Then I said, 'Randy, you can't be serious. This is the twenty-first century. No intelligent, educated person believes there really is a devil. You don't really believe that, do you?'" Then our conversation continued like this:

"Well, my parents taught me that there is, but I have always had doubts about it."

"That's a good start," I said. "Think about it, Randy. Have

you ever seen the devil?"

"No."

"Do you know anyone who says he saw the devil?"

"Well, no."

"How about your parents? Did they ever tell you that they saw the devil?"

"No."

"Hey guys, anyone here ever seen the devil?"

They all laughed. Randy turned red.

"Okay. Okay. I don't think there is a real devil as such, but bad things do happen to people," Randy said.

"Well, yeah," I said, "but that's not proof that there is a devil. In fact, if anything, maybe that's proof that there is no God, since a good God wouldn't let bad things happen."

"Excellent," interjected the Boss. "You handled that very well. In fact, you hit on a very important point. Not only do we want people to believe there is no devil, we want them to believe that there is no God."

"Yes, sir. Thank you, sir," Jonathan replied.

"We need to discuss that in much more detail later, but first I have an assignment for you. As you have been taught, even most preachers almost never mention the devil anymore. They talk about sin and all that, but our efforts at ridicule by the news media, thought leaders, professors of religion, and others have been so successful that even preachers shy away from talking about the devil.

"However, it has come to my attention that there is a fire-and-brimstone preacher in a small church in Metropolis. We cannot let this continue. Others may be encouraged to start talking about the devil and what he does. This is a very dangerous threat to our success.

"Your assignment is to go put a stop to this. As you know, you cannot kill him. You must use our tools of deception and deceit to destroy him. He is a very pious man, and I can tell you that some of our best methods—sex, financial greed, and lust for power have already been tried and have failed in this case.

"Now go. And do not come back until you can report that you have been successful." With that, the Boss pointed to the door, and Jonathan withdrew with a look of concern on his face.

Chapter 2

)) The Fire-and-Brimstone Preacher–Part One

Now what? thought Jonathan. *If I can do this, I am well on my way to being the Boss's apprentice. If I fail …* Jonathan blocked the thought from his mind. He had heard the stories about others who had let the Boss down. He did not want to go there.

Lacking a plan, Jonathan decided he would start by attending Pastor Smith's church service the next Sunday and see if that would offer some clue as to how he might proceed.

The next Sunday, Jonathan arrived at the church. It was a relatively small church in a middle-class part of the town. After saying hello to the greeter, he took a seat in the back of the sanctuary and carefully observed the proceedings.

There were about 200 people in the church, Jonathan

estimated, as the service began.

After a welcome, announcements, some singing, and a prayer by an elder of the church, Pastor Smith began his sermon.

He began with the story of Eve and the snake in the Garden of Eden.

I wonder why she wasn't afraid of the snake, Jonathan thought. He made a mental note to ask the Boss about it—if he ever saw him again. Jonathan couldn't help but admire how the Boss had convinced her that eating the fruit would make her like a god—knowing good and evil.

It's a good thing that people are never satisfied with what they have, Jonathan thought. *Eve had everything—a beautiful place to live, plenty to eat, never hot, never cold, no crime, no wars, no sickness, and a husband who loved her. But the Boss understood people always want more. In Eve's case the only thing she did not have was being a goddess. So that's what the Boss promised her! And it worked!*

Jonathan still had trouble understanding how a snake could be more persuasive than the One Whose Name We Do Not Speak (OWNWDNS) who Eve had seen face-to-face, but Jonathan credited it to the Boss's ability to spot a weakness and the Boss's extraordinary ability to convince people of his wisdom and sincerity and concern for them.

The sermon went on: about how the devil is real and is active in our world today. About how the devil uses greed, sexual desire, lust for power, jealousy, and so forth to ruin people's lives.

After the service, Jonathan mingled with the congregation

to find out what the people thought about Pastor Smith and his sermon.

To Jonathan's dismay, many in the congregation agreed with what Pastor Smith had said and seemed very devoted to him. On the other hand, there were a few who confided to Jonathan that all this talk about the devil was really out of place. They were concerned that the pastor's sermon might be causing some of the wealthier members of the congregation to look for a church elsewhere. That, in turn, would leave the church in a financial bind.

At the church door, Pastor Smith stood shaking hands and visiting with people as they left.

Pastor Smith greeted Jonathan with a warm smile and a strong handshake.

"Welcome to our church, young man. What's your name?" asked the pastor.

"Jonathan," he replied. "I really liked your sermon today," Jonathan said with a straight face.

"Oh, thank you. It really needs to be said, but I am afraid that some of our members are uncomfortable with the message. Are you new in town?" the pastor asked.

"Yes, I just moved in from down under," Jonathan said.

Jonathan noticed that the pastor had deep bags under his eyes and gave every indication of being very tired.

"Are you feeling all right, Pastor? You look a little tired," Jonathan said.

"Yes, between visiting the sick, counseling some couples who are considering divorce, visiting the prison, raising money, and caring for my own family, I am a bit exhausted," the pastor said. "But I really love my work, spreading the gospel."

This gave Jonathan an idea.

"What's your line of work?" Pastor Smith asked.

"I do medical research. I moved here recently to work with the Metropolis Good Samaritan Hospital," Jonathan said. "I have to go now, but if you're interested, perhaps I can tell you a bit about it next Sunday after church," Jonathan said.

"I would be delighted," Pastor Smith said. Then he turned his attention to a few of the church members still milling around outside the church.

Jonathan had a busy week making arrangements to make sure that Pastor Smith would have an exhausting week and was back in church the following Sunday.

After enduring another sermon, Jonathan greeted Pastor Smith as he left the church. As Jonathan had hoped, the pastor looked extremely tired.

"Hello, Pastor. That was another great sermon. I really liked it," Jonathan lied. "Are you feeling all right, Pastor? You look sort of tired."

"Yes, I am tired. I don't know what happened. It seems like all of a sudden, half of the congregation is sick. The two other prison chaplains had family emergencies out of town, so I had to fill in for them. Then I had to counsel a couple whose daughter ran away from home. They need me so much, but I don't know how I can keep it up!"

"I'm very sorry to hear that, Pastor. Perhaps I can help. As I mentioned last week, I am doing medical research at the Metropolis Good Samaritan Hospital. We are testing an experimental drug that improves a person's energy level without any side effects. We need a few more volunteers to test the drug before we submit the results to the FDA for approval. Would you like to help us out? It sounds like it is something that you might need right now," Jonathan said.

"Oh, I don't know. I really don't like to take any medication unless I really need it," Pastor Smith said.

"Sure, I understand," Jonathan said. "But you look so tired, and so many people are counting on you, that I wanted to help if I could. If you change your mind, just let me know."

"Well, maybe you are right. Are you sure this is all approved and there are no side effects that you know of?" the pastor asked.

"That's what our research has shown so far," Jonathan said.

"Okay. I'll give it a try. I have so many people I have to see this week."

"I have some paperwork here I need you to sign that says you understand that this is an experimental drug and you consent and so forth. Then here is a thirty-day supply of pills. If you feel any side effects or have any problems, please call me immediately. However, based on our very promising results so far, I don't think you will have any problems. Here is my phone number if you need to contact me for any reason."

"God bless you!" said the pastor, sending a shiver down Jonathan's spine.

The pills worked great. Pastor Smith never had so much energy or felt so good. *It really is a great medication,* the pastor thought.

For the next several days, Pastor Smith served his congregation with energy and compassion. Then one afternoon there was a knock on his church office door. He opened the door and was greeted by two police officers.

"We are sorry to trouble you, Pastor, but we have had reports that you are using, and may be dealing, in illegal drugs. Do you mind if we look around?" Sergeant Thomas said.

"No. But I assure you, those reports are wrong. The only drug I have is an experimental drug being tested at the Metropolis Good Samaritan Hospital," Pastor Smith said.

"Can I see it?" Sergeant Thomas asked.

"Sure, here are the pills."

"Do you have any more of these?"

"No, just this thirty-day supply."

"Do you mind if I look in your desk?"

"No. Go ahead. There's nothing there."

Sergeant Thomas opened a desk drawer and pulled out a bag that appeared to contain several thousand pills.

"What's this?" the Sergeant asked.

"I have no idea. I never saw those before," stammered Pastor Smith.

"We will have to test them, but based on my experience they are probably methamphetamine. Because of the large amount, you could be facing several years in prison, Pastor. I am very sorry, but I need to read you your Miranda rights and take you into the station for processing," Sergeant Thomas said.

Jonathan knocked on the Boss's door.

"Come in, come in."

Jonathan opened the door.

"Have a seat, Jonathan. I just finished reading your report on Pastor Smith. Brilliantly done. His only weakness was a desire to serve his congregation, and you exploited it wonderfully," the Boss said.

"Thanks, Boss. Studying your methods at the Academy was what inspired me," Jonathan replied, suppressing a mild feeling of guilt, which Jonathan found very disturbing.

Chapter 3

)) The Fire-and-Brimstone Preacher–Part Two

"Many prayers have come up to me for Pastor Smith. Your assignment is to go help him."

"Yes, Sir," said Angelica. "Do you have any specific directions for me?"

"You will know what to do when you get there."

Angelica soon found herself outside of the jail where Pastor Smith was incarcerated.

Angelica looked to be about twenty-five years old. She had a quiet beauty and a gentle smile. She was dressed in blue jeans and a white sweater.

Well, thought Angelica to herself, *I suppose the first thing I should do is visit Pastor Smith, try to comfort him, and see what he has to say.*

She entered the lobby of the jail. There, in an adjoining

room behind a bulletproof glass window, sat the receptionist.

"Hello," said Angelica. "I am here to visit Pastor Smith."

"Visiting hours end in half an hour, so you will have to be quick about it," the receptionist replied. "Are you an attorney?"

"No," Angelica replied.

"In that case, you will be in a separate room with a glass window between you. There is an intercom between the two rooms. Your conversation will be recorded," the receptionist instructed.

Angelica was led into a small room. Pastor Smith soon appeared on the other side of the glass.

"Hello, Pastor. I'm Angelica Johnson," Angelica said gently.

For a moment, Pastor Smith thought he saw a bright light around Angelica, but it faded quickly, and he thought it must have been his eyes adjusting to different lighting conditions.

"Have we met before, Angelica? Do I know you?"

"No, Pastor, we haven't met. But I heard about your situation and came to see if I could help," Angelica said.

"Well, I appreciate it, but I don't see how you can help. I'm afraid that I was tricked into violating the law."

"What happened, Pastor?"

"About a week ago a young man who had attended my church a few times noticed that I was tired. He said he was doing medical research at Metropolis Good Samaritan Hospital. He said they were testing a new experimental drug that would improve a person's energy level without any side effects. He asked if I would like to volunteer to help with the test.

"I was somewhat reluctant, but I had so many people who needed my help, and I was so tired that I agreed to use it. I had no idea it was an illegal drug. In fact, he had me sign a paper that said I understood it was an experimental drug and that I was assuming the risk and so forth."

"Do you have a copy of that paper?" Angelica asked.

"Well, as a matter fact, he must've dropped it as he left. I found it on the floor later that day and put it in my desk drawer so that I could give it to him the next time he came to church. It's still in the desk drawer as far as I know."

"Did you get his name?"

"Just his first name. It was Jonathan."

"What did he look like?"

"Well, he was a young man, probably in his twenties. Brown hair, blue eyes, about six feet tall. He appeared to have an athletic build. Probably weighs about 160 pounds. Nicely dressed in a blue suit and red tie when I saw him in church."

"Do you lock your church office when you're away, Pastor?"

"No. I never saw the need. There isn't too much of value there."

"Do you have surveillance cameras at the church or in your office?"

"No, the church council considered it a while ago, but there was no money available to go ahead with it."

"I understand that when you were arrested the police

found a bag of pills in your desk."

"Yes. I have no idea how those got there," the pastor said.

"Do you have a lawyer, Pastor?"

"My, you certainly have a lot of questions, Ms. Johnson. Who do you work for and why are you here?" Pastor Smith asked with some suspicion in his voice.

"The denomination superiors heard of your situation and sent me to help you," Angelica assured him.

"Well, all right. Thank you. A young woman in the congregation just out of law school has volunteered to help me. She is coming to see me tomorrow for our first meeting," the pastor said.

"Would it be okay with you if I talked to her?" Angelica asked.

"Certainly, if you wish. Her name is Esther MacDonald. Her office is just down the street from the church."

"Time's up," the corrections officer announced. And with that, Angelica was escorted from the building.

I think I will look over the church and then go see the lawyer, Angelica thought to herself.

When she arrived at the church, she found that it was unlocked, and she went inside.

"Hello, is anyone here?" she said in a loud voice.

There was no answer.

She made her way to the pastor's office and went in. The pastor's desk was in the middle of the room. She went over to it and opened the center drawer. There was the experimental drug consent form.

I'm sure the pastor wouldn't mind if I took this to his attorney, Angelica thought to herself. So she put it in the briefcase she was carrying and left the church.

Upon leaving the church, Angelica noticed a pawnshop across the street from the church with a security camera clearly visible and pointing directly at the church.

Angelica wondered if, by chance, there was a video of this Jonathan person that had been captured by the pawnshop security camera.

I think I will stop in there and ask the pawnshop owner if he has video from a few weeks ago and if he would let me see it, Angelica said to herself.

As she entered the pawnshop, Angelica saw a middle-aged woman behind the counter.

"Are you, by any chance, the owner of the store?" Angelica asked.

"Yes, I am. What can I do for you?" the woman replied.

"I'm trying to help Pastor Smith, the pastor in the church across the street. Do you know him by any chance?" Angelica asked.

"As a matter fact, I do. I am a member of that church," the woman replied. "I never would've believed that Pastor Smith was a drug dealer! He seems like such a nice man."

"Yes, he does," Angelica replied. "The denomination superiors have sent me to see if I can help him. They believe that he is innocent."

"Well, it's sad to say, but the police caught him red-handed," the woman replied.

"Yes, I know it looks bad. But you would want to help him if you could, wouldn't you?"

"Yes, of course. I have been praying for him. But many of the church members think we need to let him go and get a new pastor."

"How long do you keep the video recordings from your security camera on the front of your store?" Angelica asked.

"Thirty days," the woman replied.

"Could you let me make a copy of the last thirty days of video? I think it might help the pastor."

"I don't see how, but you are welcome to make a copy if you think it would help," the woman replied.

With a copy of the video in hand, Angelica next went to the law office of Esther MacDonald.

"Be with you in a minute," said a pleasant voice from an office adjacent to the reception area.

While Angelica waited, she looked around at the reception area. It was neat and tidy but sparsely furnished. Ms. McDonald's framed law degree hung on one wall. On another wall was a quote from the Bible: *He has showed you, O man, what is good; and what does the Lord require of you but to do justice, and to love kindness, and to walk humbly with your God? Micah 6:8[1]*

"Sorry to keep you waiting. How can I be of service?" Esther asked.

"My name is Angelica. The denomination superiors sent me to help Pastor Smith," Angelica said. "He told me that you are his lawyer."

"Yes, I'm going to try and help him. He probably told you

that I am a recent law school graduate and I just opened this law office a few months ago."

"He did say something about that," Angelica replied.

"I haven't had a chance to speak to Pastor Smith in detail yet, but I have reviewed the police report, and it looks like a very difficult case to defend," Esther said.

"Maybe I can help. I've done some investigating, and I believe I have strong evidence that Pastor Smith was framed," Angelica said.

"Really? And what is the evidence?" Esther asked.

"A young man by the name of Jonathan, last name unknown, asked the pastor to participate in an experimental drug research project. He had the pastor sign a waiver form that basically said that this is an experimental drug being researched by Metropolis Good Samaritan Hospital. As it happened, this Jonathan person dropped the waiver form when he left the pastor's office, so I have that form with me," said Angelica, giving the document to Esther.

"Does this Jonathan work for the hospital?" Esther asked.

"No, I checked that out. They never heard of him, and they are not researching an experimental drug," Angelica replied.

"Why would this Jonathan person lie about this and give the pastor methamphetamine pills?" Esther asked.

"That, I don't know for sure. Some people are just evil, I guess."

"So we don't know his motive?" Esther replied.

"No, but I do have a video of him entering the church with what appears to be a bag of pills the day the pastor was arrested. That same video shows the pastor leaving the church several minutes prior to Jonathan entering the church. So it looks like Jonathan waited until he was sure no one was around before he took the pills in," Angelica explained.

"May I have a copy of the video, please?" Esther asked excitedly.

"That's why I brought it here."

"Where did you get it?"

"From the pawnshop owner across the street. It was from her camera."

"This is wonderful," Esther exclaimed. "With this evidence and Pastor Smith's good reputation, I think I can persuade the district attorney to drop the felony intent-to-deliver charges and agree to pretrial diversion on the misdemeanor possession charges."

"I'm glad I was able to help," Angelica said with a smile.

Back at home, Angelica was ushered into His presence.

"Well done, good and faithful servant. Pastor Smith has been set free and is once again serving his congregation."

"Thank you, Sir," Angelica beamed.

Chapter 4

)) The Creation in Six Days Nonsense

"What did they teach you at the Academy about this 'everything was created in six days' business?" the Boss asked.

"We spent a lot of time on that, Boss. They emphasized how important it is and how easy it is to convince people that this was impossible and never really happened," Jonathan said.

The Boss looked at him intently and asked, "Did they explain why this is so important?"

"Yes, sir. If people believe that OWNWDNS could really do this, then they would necessarily also believe that he is very powerful. And if they believe that, then they would be much more likely to obey his rules, which would make our job much more difficult," Jonathan explained, just as he had been taught at the Academy.

"And what are tools we use for convincing people that the 'creation in six days' business is just a fairytale?"

"Ridicule and logic, sir", Jonathan replied.

"Go on," the Boss said.

"In this case ridicule and logic fit together perfectly. The human mind cannot really comprehend the idea that everything on earth, and the universe itself, was created out of nothing by a supreme being. And even many of those who think that everything might have been created by a supreme being can't believe that it could be done in six days. And because it sounds so impossible, it is easy to get people to laugh at the few who believe it and to question their intelligence," Jonathan said.

"There is another reason the issue is so important. What is that reason?" the Boss asked, studying Jonathan intently.

"Because if people believe that the first story in the Bible is untrue, then they will have doubts about the accuracy of everything else in the Bible, and half of our work is already done for us," Jonathan replied.

The Boss nodded his approval. "Tell me about your in-service training on this issue."

"Yes, sir. I had a very challenging assignment. I was sent to an evangelical seminary as a student and took a class on creationism," Jonathan said.

"Go on."

"One day in class I said to the professor, 'Sir, almost every scientist says there is scientific proof that the earth is billions of years old, and that dinosaurs lived millions of years ago. When I have my own ministry, what am I supposed to say about this?'"

The professor said, "Tell them what Hebrews 11:1 says.

This is a question of faith and that 'faith is an assurance of things hoped for, the conviction of things not seen."[2]

"I understand faith," I said. "But in this case the indisputable scientific facts are that the earth is billions of years old and that life evolved over a long period of time. Am I supposed to have faith that science has it all wrong?" I asked.

"To make a long story short, the professor did not have a very good answer to that question. After class, several other students confided to me that they had the same question and doubts but were afraid it might hurt their grade in the class if they said anything. They said they admired my courage in speaking up," Jonathan said with a laugh.

"Well done," the Boss said. "I can see why you were first in your class at the Academy."

"Sir, I do have a question that they weren't able to answer at the Academy."

"Go on."

"Well, it seems to me that there are three possibilities. One, that the earth and the universe were created by OWNWDNS in six days. Two, that it was created by OWNWDNS over billions of years. And three, that it all happened as a result of random chance over a period of billions of years," Jonathan said.

"So, what is your question?" the Boss said, appearing to be somewhat annoyed at Jonathan's statement.

"Well, sir, why do people find it easier to believe that all of the stars and galaxies and planets, the extraordinarily complex human DNA, and human eyes and ears and brain are the result of random chance instead of design? And why is it easier to believe that some methane, nitrogen, water, and a few other chemicals that had never been alive, for no reason at all except random chance, came to life as a living cell?" Jonathan asked.

The Boss frowned. "This is not something we usually discuss. However, since you may soon be my apprentice, I will make an exception this one time. But you are never to speak of this again. Is that clear?"

"Yes, sir."

"Part of the answer is that most people just don't think deeply about this. And we don't want them to. With my help, people are constantly reminded how ridiculous it is to claim that everything was created in six days. For most people that is just not believable, and people who do believe it are ridiculed and laughed at.

"What they don't think about is the extraordinary statistical improbability that the complex DNA of a human being—or other life forms—was formed by random chance. They don't think about the fact that no scientist has ever taken the known chemicals of life and created even the simplest living cell in a laboratory. Being intellectually lazy, they are content to think vaguely that over billions of years pretty much anything could happen by random chance. Our job—your job, Jonathan—is to continue to encourage this kind of thinking," the Boss emphasized.

"Yes, sir."

"Sir, did you see the recent scientific article that the speed of light is not a constant and that at creation the speed of light was much faster than today? Therefore, the measurements of the age of the universe based on the speed of light are wrong and the universe is much younger than was previously thought?"

At this, the Boss became visibly angry. "Yes," he snapped. "And I will be doing everything I can to discredit those scientists and that study. I'm sure you understand how dangerous this is to us. If the scientists start agreeing that their studies show that the universe is not billions of years old, that gives tremendous credibility to this 'creation in six days' nonsense," the Boss shouted.

Jonathan did not know what to say. He had obviously made the Boss very angry. *Now what?* thought Jonathan.

"Sir, I'm sure you will be able to put a stop to this. What can I do to help?"

"Let me give that some thought," the Boss replied.

Chapter 5

)) A Mistake?

Jonathan thought it best to change the subject. "Sir, you have done so many amazing things. Your performance in the Garden of Eden got the ball rolling on everything evil. And getting the Israelites to make that golden calf in the desert was very impressive."

"Yes," the Boss beamed, "that was really something. They'd seen all those plagues Moses brought forth—turning the river to blood, the locusts, the flies, the frogs, and the death of all the Egyptian firstborn. They'd seen the parting of the Red Sea and the death of Pharaoh's entire army. And after seeing all those miracles, I was still able to turn them away from OWNWDNS in less than forty days after Moses went up the mountain. Not only that, it was Moses' own brother who made the calf!" the Boss chortled.

"Yes, Boss. That was very impressive. Compared to that, turning people away from OWNWDNS today must almost seem like child's play to you," Jonathan purred.

"Well, I just make it look easy," the Boss grinned.

"Has there ever been anything you wish you had done differently?" Jonathan asked.

"Well, I don't make many mistakes," the Boss replied. "But I did make one big one."

"What was that?" Jonathan asked.

"Persecuting the early followers of that—that—Son. That was a huge mistake."

"My intent had been to frighten the early followers into giving up their new religion. I thought that the fear of torture and death would at least cause them to publicly renounce their faith and stop talking about the Son and recruiting others, even if they secretly continued to believe it themselves," the Boss said.

"Instead, in response to the persecution, many of the early followers of the Son fled to other countries and took their new religion with them. So my effort to stamp out the new religion before it could take hold actually led to the spread of it," the Boss said disgustedly.

"What I should've done then was to use ridicule and logic, as we do today. For example, after first making the case that there is no God, we say that, even if there were, his Son, if he had one, would be another God, not a human. And if the Son were a man, a good, loving, and powerful God would not allow his own Son to be tortured to death. And, of course, it is utter nonsense to think that a dead person could come back to life. That's how I should've handled it, and we wouldn't have all these Christian churches around today," the Boss sighed.

Chapter 6

)) The Rules Changed

"But do you know what really makes me angry about OWNWDNS's Son?" the Boss asked.

"What, sir?" Jonathan asked.

"That's when OWNWDNS changed the rules. Up until the Son came along, if people didn't follow OWNWDNS's commandments, I usually got to keep their souls. But now, all they have to do is believe in the Son and ask for forgiveness, and I'm out. It's not fair, it's not fair at all, but it's what I've come to expect. Even before the Son came along, OWNWDNS had a history of letting people off who rightfully belonged to me," the Boss said angrily.

"Do you mean, for instance, Abraham, Moses, and David?" Jonathan asked, relying on what he had been taught at the Academy.

"Yes, exactly," said the Boss. "Take Abraham for instance. Of course, he came before the Ten Commandments and all those other laws, but still. Abraham was a guy who basically prostituted his wife in order to make himself rich. And it did make him rich! That's my kind of guy! He should have been mine!" the Boss exclaimed.

"But oh, no. OWNWDNS gives him a pass because Abraham believed in Him, and get this: it was 'credited to him as righteousness.'[3] Give me a break. I do everything right. I put this idea of prostituting his wife in Abraham's head, and he does it not once but twice. He should be here with us right now. It just isn't fair," the Boss complained.

"And then there was that guy Moses. A murderer, that's what he was. He killed the Egyptian before he fled from Egypt. It was murder, pure and simple. He should by rights be with us, too. But oh, no. OWNWDNS makes him into the greatest hero in Jewish history. It's just not right. What about 'Thou shalt not kill' and all that?" the Boss complained.

"One of the most outrageous deals was King David. By then OWNWDNS had given those Ten Commandments and a bunch of other laws. So David knew what was right and what was wrong.

"And he had everything that a man could want. He was wealthy beyond belief. He had hundreds of wives and concubines. He had cattle and horses too numerous to count. He had a powerful army at his beck and call. But that wasn't enough for David. Oh no.

"Since he already had so much, he was a real challenge for me. But I had an idea—a woman of extraordinary beauty to tempt him with.

"As you know, I put the thought of taking a nude bath

on the top of her house, where David could see her, in Bathsheba's head. But, of course, I can only suggest things. I can't make people do what I want. They have to make that decision themselves. And she did. She wanted to be a queen."

"Well, things worked even better than I had hoped. First, there was coveting his neighbor's wife, and then the adultery—from which she became pregnant with David's child.

"Next came the deceit. David ordered Bathsheba's husband, Uriah, home from the army so that Uriah would have sex with his wife and Uriah would think that the child was his. But Uriah refused to lay with his wife while his comrades were in the field fighting a war.

"Next, David arranged for Uriah to be killed in battle. We would call it murder.

"Then, with Uriah dead, David took Bathsheba to be his wife. In essence, he stole her—the same as if he had taken Uriah's money or his horse or whatever after he had him killed.

"At this point I was sure that David would be mine—for all eternity. I mean, coveting his neighbor's wife, adultery, deceit, murder, and theft. That's violating five of the Ten Commandments right there! By OWNWDNS's own rules, David was supposed to belong to me," the Boss complained.

"But, oh no. OWNWDNS gave David a pass. Sure, there were some adverse consequences, but David's second son by Bathsheba went on to be king, and David lived to a ripe old age. And to add insult to injury, OWNWDNS's Son was a descendent of David! Where is the justice in that?" the

Boss asked.

"That's when I should've seen it coming—OWNWDNS forgiving people as bad as David if they believed in Him and asked for forgiveness.

"Now with the Son forgiving sins if a person believes in him, our job is a lot harder. Not only do we have to tempt them into violating the rules, we have to keep them from believing in the Son and asking for forgiveness," the Boss complained.

"Yes, Boss, but you have done a great job just the same," Jonathan replied.

"Well, yes, I have, if I do say so myself," the Boss said. And I am encouraged by one thing the Son said: 'For the gate is wide and the way is easy, that leads to destruction, and those who enter by it are many. For the gate is narrow and the way is hard, that leads to life, and those who find it are few.'⁴ He got that right. I do everything I can to make it easy to get here and a great many have entered our gates," the Boss said with satisfaction.

Chapter 7

)) The Rules

"We're lucky that so many people don't understand the purpose of the rules and don't understand that not only am I interested in their souls, I want to make their lives as miserable as possible while they're alive too," the Boss explained.

"Yes, sir. We studied that in our legal studies class at the Academy," Jonathan volunteered.

"Go on."

"The basic purpose of many of OWNWDNS's rules is to prevent conflict between people that leads to anger and unhappiness and revenge. In other words, many of the rules are intended to make life on earth a more pleasant, happier experience.

"Of course," Jonathan added, "we like to tell people that OWNWDNS's rules are there because OWNWDNS doesn't want people to have any fun."

"Correct," the Boss said. "Please continue with your

explanation of what you learned about each rule at the Academy."

"Yes, sir.

"Let me begin with the rule that a person should not murder another person. Killing a person obviously makes friends and the family of the murdered person sad and angered at the murderer. In the old days, it was common for the family of the murdered person to take revenge by killing or kidnapping or raping members of the murderer's family. Even today that is common in some societies. And in the United States, criminal gangs still do that," Jonathan explained as he had been taught at the Academy.

"The rule about not stealing has somewhat the same purpose but in some ways is even more fundamental to a flourishing society," he continued.

"Over time, if theft is widespread, many people see no purpose in working. That is pretty easy to understand. For example, if you are a farmer and all of your crops and live-stock will be taken away from you by a thief year after year, then why continue farming?

"Or if you are a furniture maker, but as soon as you finish each piece of furniture it is taken from you by a thief time after time, why would the furniture maker continue to make furniture?"

"Well said, Jonathan," said the Boss. "That's why I love socialism. While technically it is not theft because it is the government that takes the fruits of a person's labor, the result is always the same eventually. People come to understand that no matter how hard or long they work, or how inventive they are, most of what they produce is being taken from them. And most of them eventually say to themselves, I can get free food, housing, medical care, and other nice things from the government without working. So they stop working. And when enough people do that, there are food shortages, housing falls into disrepair, water systems fail, electrical energy and gasoline become in short supply, and so forth."

"Then when these desperate people challenge their government and demand change, the reaction of the government is usually to brutally suppress the complainers using the secret police and the military.

"That is exactly what is happening in Venezuela today. But it was the same thing with the Soviet Union and other socialist and communist countries. It is always the same, because human nature is always the same. And I am an expert on human nature," the Boss grinned.

"Yes, sir," Jonathan replied. "Would you like me to go on about what we learned about the rules at the Academy?" Jonathan asked.

"Yes. I want to be sure the professors at the Academy are teaching things exactly the way I have instructed them. So please continue."

"Yes, sir. Well, another rule of OWNWDNS is not to lie. Lying can cause innocent persons to go to prison, but the more common result of lying is that it makes the person lied to angry or heartbroken when they find out.

"For example, there is fraud. There are many different schemes. Such as, a grandparent is told by the scammer that her grandson is in jail in Canada and she must wire money to the scammer, who claims to be a Canadian official, to get her grandson out.

"One of the best and most frequently used lies is the age-old one of the young man who professes his love for his girlfriend to achieve his objective. Then, he is nowhere to be found after she becomes pregnant.

"Then there is the rule about not being jealous of what your neighbor has—his house, his car, his country club membership, and so forth. This rule is designed primarily for the benefit of the person, not the neighbor. Because desiring what someone else has that you don't have can make a person unhappy or depressed. It can also lead to theft or vandalism."

"Yes," said the Boss. "And when it comes to breaking this rule, the politicians lead the pack.

"'Vote *for me*,' they say, 'and I will tax the rich because they should not have more than you do. And I will nationalize the means of production. I will take the railroads, and the oil fields, and the other businesses away from the rich and turn them over to you,' they say.

"Sometimes it's called Marxism or communism or socialism or whatever. But it works for many of the politicians because so many people let themselves be jealous of what others have.

"What I don't like about free enterprise is that it takes the human desire to have more than others and channels it for good purposes. Under the free enterprise model, to be successful a person has to provide something that other people want to have and will voluntarily pay for.

"So Bill Gates, Jeff Bezos, and others like them did not get rich by stealing from others. They each provided something people wanted to have and voluntarily paid for.

"One nice thing about rich people is that most of them wind up here with us. As the Son said, 'It is easier for a camel to go through the eye of a needle than for a rich man to go to heaven.'"[5]

"Why is that, Boss?" Jonathan asked.

"Didn't you study that at the Academy?" the Boss asked sharply.

"No, sir. Our instructor just said it pretty much takes care of itself," Jonathan said defensively.

"Well, I will have to have a word with your instructor," the Boss said, somewhat annoyed.

"Although there are various reasons, it is that our tools work as well with the rich as they do anyone else—oftentimes even better," the Boss explained.

"The temptation of adultery works particularly well with rich men. Their money attracts a lot of women who hope to gain some of that wealth and power. For example, Bathsheba and King David, John F. Kennedy, Jeff Bezos, Tiger Woods—the list goes on and on."

"Do we get all of the rich people?" Jonathan asked.

"No, if they believe in the Son and ask for forgiveness, we lose them, just like everyone else. So we miss a few."

"Yes, sir. Do you want me to do the adultery rule next?" Jonathan asked.

"Yes, by all means."

"A married man having sex with a woman who is not his wife, or a married woman having sex with a man who is not her husband, almost always results in extreme anger and heartbreak. Very often, it leads to divorce."

"I want to talk about that more later on when we discuss the Internet," the Boss said.

"Yes, sir," Jonathan replied.

Chapter 8

))Breakdown of the Family

"Perhaps the project I'm most proud of in recent years is the breakdown of the family in the United States," the Boss said with a smile.

"I made it look easy, but it was really quite a challenge. When I started on the project, adultery was a criminal offense in many states. And getting a divorce was difficult. The husband or wife had to go to court and prove sexual infidelity or cruelty or whatever. And there was strong social and religious pressure against divorce.

"And not only that, there was strong social pressure, if a young man got a girl pregnant, that he marry her and care for her and their child. They were called shotgun weddings, although in fact the girl's father only rarely actually used a shotgun!" the Boss laughed.

"All of that was a lot to overcome. But I came up with a plan and put the necessary ideas into the heads of opinion leaders and some politicians who I thought might be helpful," the Boss beamed.

"As usual, I relied heavily on logic and compassion to win the day. For example, I suggested having to prove fault in a divorce didn't really prevent divorce. It just required putting all the family's dirty laundry on display in the courtroom. It was cruel to both the spouses and especially their poor children who are exposed to very embarrassing disclosures about their parents. And, of course, the children were then often subjected to ridicule at school.

"I also promoted the argument that anyone who really wanted a divorce could eventually get one by being cruel enough to the spouse or by simply lying since there were usually only two people who knew the truth.

"So the logical answer to all of this was the idea of no-fault divorce. No longer did one spouse have to prove the other spouse was a bad person to get a divorce. They just had to say that the marriage was 'irretrievably broken'— whatever that means. They and their children were spared public humiliation from the disclosure of family secrets. No longer did a spouse have to be cruel to the other spouse in order to force a divorce.

"So with logic and compassion I carried the day," the Boss laughed. "No-fault divorce is a great illustration of one of my favorite sayings—'The road to hell is paved with good intentions!'[6]

"And, of course, there were additional benefits as time went on. Since divorces were no longer anyone's fault and since some of the dirty laundry never became public in most divorces, gradually the social stigma of divorce dissipated.

In fact, today, while most people would say that divorce is unfortunate, many people view divorce, especially by other people, as no big deal. In fact, someone once said that it's easier to get out of a marriage than it is to get out of a cell phone contract!

"The ease of no-fault divorce and lack of public stigma have greatly increased divorce. Today the divorce rate in the United States is almost double what it was in 1960. In fact, today in the United States almost fifty percent of all marriages will end in divorce or separation.

"Divorce really does so much for us," the Boss continued.

"You get the emotional pain of divorce on the couple, their parents and siblings and, of course, the children—who often feel guilty, thinking that the divorce was somehow their fault.

"Often divorce or unwed motherhood results in children growing up in fatherless homes. In fact, forty-three percent of US children now live without a father in the home. And the chances that children from fatherless homes will get in trouble with the law, use illegal drugs, do poorly in school, and get divorced themselves someday increase dramatically," the Boss said with great satisfaction.

"Did they teach you at the Academy that eighty-five percent of all youths in prison come from fatherless homes? Seventy-one percent of all high school dropouts come from fatherless homes. Seventy-five percent of all adolescent patients in chemical abuse centers come from fatherless homes. Eighty-five percent of all children who have behavior disorders come from fatherless homes. Seventy-one percent of pregnant teenagers don't have a father in the home. My statistics department is really on top of this!" the Boss bragged.

"They sure are, Boss, and they also taught us that widespread divorce weakens the institution of marriage so that it is no longer seen as a lifetime commitment but more like friends sharing a living arrangement for a period of time.

"And since it seems that way, more and more young people do just that—share a living arrangement for a period of time. They don't get married at all! 'Friends with benefits' they call it! You gotta love that," Jonathan said laughing.

"Right. And so along comes a baby and the father decides it's time to find a new friend, and we get more single-parent families!" the Boss exclaimed.

"And then, as I mentioned previously, there used to be social pressure for a guy to marry a girl if she got pregnant. That pressure has largely gone away.

"But three other important factors in the breakdown of the family in the United States were birth control, abortion, and social welfare programs.

"Now I want to be clear," the Boss said. "I did not invent those things, but I immediately saw their potential.

"Once again, it was just logic and compassion. A lot of single guys agreed with my concept—it was the girl's responsibility to use birth control. If she didn't and she got pregnant, she could get an abortion. So from the guy's logical standpoint, there was no child he was responsible for. It was all up to the girl. If she wanted the child and he didn't— well, that was her problem. He certainly had no reason to marry her, unless he really wanted to.

"So this kind of thinking has increased the number of out-of-wedlock births dramatically. In the United States out-of-wedlock births increased from five percent in 1960 to forty percent of all live births today!

"Another big plus for us in the United States were the social welfare programs such as aid to dependent children and food stamps. Those programs made it more feasible for an unmarried woman to make ends meet. And just as importantly, some of those programs were only available to women who were not married. And the more children they had, the more financial support they got from the government. This provided an incentive for both men and women not to marry when a woman was pregnant.

"And then we had the feminists who made the case that men are not needed. Some even said that all men are rapists or toxic. So more and more men came to the conclusion that if a woman thought he was not needed, he was happy to leave the pregnant woman and find a new lover.

"And, to my pleasant surprise, even the Son's church has largely acquiesced in divorce. The Catholic Church was about the last holdout. They still say that divorce is wrong since the Son said so, but then they hand out annulments by the bushel basket. It used to be that an annulment was given only when a marriage had not been consummated— that is, the happy couple had never had sex with each other. But now people married thirty years with kids can get an annulment from the church. I never dreamed I could be so successful with divorce," the Boss confided.

Chapter 9

)) Collapse of Society

"A great way to create mass misery and bring many more souls our way is the complete collapse of a society," the Boss commented.

"What do you mean, Boss?" Jonathan asked.

"Well, it's not easy to do. It takes a lot of time and preparation, but the rewards are great.

"There are two basic things that keep a civilized society civilized. One is laws that are enforced with penalties. For example, in the United States today, robbery is usually punished by imprisonment for a period of time. Most people don't want to go to prison, so they don't commit robbery.

"The other thing that keeps a civilized society civilized is morality. In other words, most people don't do certain things because they believe them to be morally wrong. For example, murder, robbery, et cetera.

"Some call it natural law. Others refer to the Ten Commandments in the Bible. Whatever it is called, it prevents people from doing certain things, whether they think they will get caught or not.

"Morality flows from religion. If there is no religion, there is no morality. The concept of morality is that some things are inherently wrong. So if there is no morality, there is nothing that is inherently wrong. If nothing is inherently wrong, the only question is, can I get away with it?" the Boss instructed.

"The key to our success is to convince people that there is no natural law and no inherent right or wrong. Some people call it 'situational ethics'—that right and wrong depend on the situation.

"Our idea, which is being picked up by a number of legal scholars, is that all law is a 'social construct.' There is no inherent right or wrong, these scholars say.

"Once this idea is widely accepted, the society is ready for collapse with all of the rewards that come to us when that happens," the Boss smiled.

"There is already evidence of our progress. For example, the Democratic National Committee passed a resolution in 2019 that said in part, '... the Democratic Party... recognizes that morals, values, and patriotism... are not necessarily reliant on having a religious worldview at all.' I couldn't have said it better if I had written it myself," the Boss laughed.

"Another example is the looting that frequently takes place after a hurricane, earthquake, or other natural disaster. Or even during and after a riot. Under those circumstances, the chances of being caught by law enforcement are relatively low. The only thing that can prevent criminal conduct is an inherent feeling of right and wrong. More and more people, thanks to us, no longer believe in a supreme law giver who always sees what they are doing and judges their actions.

"Imagine what would happen today in the United States, for example, if a computer hacker were to shut down the electrical grid nationwide for an extended period of time. And I want you to know that I've been putting that thought into certain peoples' minds for a while now.

"There would be no streetlights. Police radios and other communications would fail after backup power supplies were depleted. ATMs would not work. Food could not be delivered. Banks could not operate. City water systems could not produce water after backup power supplies were depleted. Since law enforcement would be very limited in its capabilities, we can expect to see widespread riots and looting and massive deaths from lack of water and food.

"Gee, Boss, is that sort of what happened with Sodom and Gomorrah?" Jonathan asked.

"Well, the principle was the same, but I didn't receive all of the benefits that were due to me," the Boss complained.

"In Sodom and Gomorrah, the people convinced them-selves, with a little help from me, that adultery, sodomy—as it is now called—bestiality, and recreational sex were per-fectly fine. In fact, they brought pleasure, which my entice-ments usually do initially.

"So things were going great. More and more people heard about what was going on and came to Sodom and Gomorrah to be part of it.

"And, of course, sexually transmitted diseases were spreading like wildfire. Not much in the way of medicines in those days. People were experiencing blindness and painful, lingering deaths. It was wonderful! And it was starting to spread outside of the cities, as people who came to Sodom and Gomorrah for the fun of it returned home. I was on a roll!" the Boss exclaimed.

"Was it like Las Vegas today, Boss?" Jonathan asked.

"No, it was much better!

"But just when things were going good, OWNWDNS stepped in. He destroyed the cities and all the people, except Lot and his family. It was outrageous. It was unfair. Sure, it brought me a bunch of souls in the short run, but if OWNWDNS hadn't stepped in, I could've spread disease and death across the whole countryside in time.

"But most of the sick people were killed, and people outside the cities were so frightened—thinking that, if they had illicit sex, they, too, would be destroyed, that it put a stop to most of it for a long time in that area," the Boss complained.

"And talk about hypocrites! OWNWDNS takes the cake. Here was Lot. First, he offered to prostitute his two daughters to save a couple of strangers. Then he winds up having sex with his two daughters. But do I get him? Oh, no. OWNWDNS forgives him. So he destroys two cities for sexual immorality, then he gives Lot a free pass for doing the same sort of things," the Boss said with disgust.

"Why, Boss?" Jonathan asked.

"I hate to even discuss it," the Boss said with a frown. "But if you must know, the difference was that the people of

Sodom and Gomorrah did not believe there was a God and did what was right in their own eyes. Lot, for all his faults, believed in God, and so he got off," the Boss explained.

"That makes our job pretty difficult, doesn't it?" Jonathan remarked.

"Yes, it does, but we have new tools available all the time we can use to our advantage," the Boss said.

Chapter 10

)) The Internet

"You mean like TV and the Internet?" Jonathan asked, remembering his communications course at the Academy.

"Yes, exactly," the Boss said. "Some people claim that I invented those, but I can't take the credit. Like many other things, they can be used for good or evil. Our job is to make sure the evil outweighs the good."

"Yes, at the Academy we studied how in its early days TV mostly promoted good," Jonathan said.

"Yes, it was pretty disgusting. The good guys always won—*The Lone Ranger* and all that. Then there were the family shows like *Leave It To Beaver* with intact families who usually did the right thing," the Boss recalled.

"Despite all that, I could see the potential in TV. It could bring glorified violence and illicit sex right into peoples' living rooms. It could portray fathers as hopeless nitwits who weren't respected by their children. It could show the joys of sex outside of marriage, while leaving out the pregnancy and the disease that follows. It could show that car chases and gun fights with police were exciting entertainment. Yes, I saw the potential right away," the Boss said.

"But nothing is easy. It took time and patience to bring all that about. One great tool was greed—the greed of the TV producers and advertisers to have the most-watched show. Another, as usual, was sex. Another was logic: 'If we don't do this, our competitors will, so we should be first.'

"Of course, as we got things rolling, some people complained to the TV stations and to the advertisers. That's where ridicule and logic were put to use.

"The argument was that the complainers were old fuddy-duddies or religious extremists who were trying to censor their fellow citizens who had a right to watch what they wanted to watch. If they didn't like what was on TV, they didn't have to watch it. That was fair. That was logical."

"It worked really well, didn't it, Boss?" Jonathan asked.

"Yes, it did. But the Internet is even better," the Boss said.

"The problem with broadcast TV is that there is still some resistance on the part of producers, and especially advertisers, to some of the things that I would like to do. We don't have that problem with the Internet."

"Yes, Boss. We studied the Internet a lot. I really like the websites dedicated to bringing together married people who want to commit adultery," Jonathan said boldly, while feeling a bit uncomfortable.

"Yes, I really couldn't have done that better if I had done it myself. Still, it builds upon the ideas I have been promoting for a long time," the Boss said.

"The website works great. Let me tell you about just one incident to give you an idea of how well it works," the Boss said.

"John had been married for twelve years and had two children, ages ten and six, with his wife, Joan. The early years of their marriage had been great. But lately John felt like Joan was so busy with her job and the children that she did not have time for him. He felt like she did not appreciate him, and they often argued over family finances. Still, he wanted to stay in the marriage for his children's sake.

"That's where I stepped in. As he was surfing the Internet, I brought his attention to a website where married persons could meet other married persons who wanted to have an adulterous relationship.

"I don't think he really wanted to have an affair," the Boss said, "but I nudged him to think that it couldn't hurt to just see what's on the website.

"Soon John came across a woman—Rachel—who was attractive and who he had a lot in common with. She had been married ten years, but her husband was so busy with his business that he had no time for her. It seemed like he was never home. He never told her anymore that he loved her or appreciated her. She had to take care of the kids almost single-handedly and longed for someone to talk to and be close to.

"John told Rachel he intended to remain faithful to his wife but that he thought they could help each other by sharing each other's burdens, so to speak.

"As time went on, they talked by phone more and more

and would meet for coffee from time to time. Over time, John developed feelings for Rachel and she for him. One thing led to another, and soon they were intimate.

"To make a long story short, their spouses eventually found out, and divorces resulted. The children were devastated, and the divorces left everyone struggling financially.

"So you can see how easy it was for me. All I had to do was bring the website to his attention, and the rest took care of itself.

"Lead them into temptation, that's my motto," the Boss laughed.

"As my apprentice you will be expected to carry on the work."

"Yes, sir," Jonathan said, feeling a little ill at ease.

Chapter 11

)) Religious Wars

"One of my favorite ways to stir up trouble, hurt people, and win souls for us is fights and atrocities in the name of religion. It's a win-win for us. We get the souls, the people feel the pain, and religion gets a bad name," the Boss said enthusiastically.

"The big deal now is the 'extreme' Muslims who want to kill the infidels. You've got to love it. The Muslims, the Jews, and the Christians all recognize Moses as a messenger of their God. And one of the commandments that their God gave through Moses was 'Thou shalt not kill.'[7] That command is in the holy book of all three religions. And yet they think they will be rewarded for killing each other!

"Did I do a great job or what!" the Boss boasted. "But that's a developing story. I suppose you studied the killing and torture that went along with the Protestant Reformation at the Academy?"

"Yes, sir," Jonathan replied.

"Well, I was there. Let me give you a brief first-hand account.

"The historians break the Wars of Reformation down into a number of individual wars. For example, the Knights' Revolt from 1522–1523, the German Peasants' War from 1524–1526, the Wars of Kappel from 1529–1531, the Tudor Conquest of Ireland from 1529–1603, and so on. I like all of them, of course—so much death, desecration, and torture! But one of my favorites was the Thirty Years' War, which I helped get started in 1618.

"The Thirty Years' War began as a war between the Protestants—mainly Lutherans—and Catholics, generally in the territory of today's Germany. In addition to those killed in battle, widespread famine and disease wiped out large numbers. Germany's population was reduced about thirty percent. During its seventeen years in Germany during the war, the Swedish army alone destroyed two thousand castles, eighteen thousand villages, and fifteen hundred towns. Large numbers of churches and monasteries were destroyed. Altogether as many as eleven million people may have died as a result of the Thirty Years' War. It was one of my most successful efforts in having Christians kill other Christians.

"On a related note, I was recently in St. Andrews, Scotland. It is a small town, but the University of St. Andrews is there. And, by the way, it is also the town where the game of golf originated.

"In the town there is a marker where a Protestant leader was burned at the stake. In another part of town there are the remains of a castle. It was, at one time, a Catholic bishop's castle. A marker there notes that the bishop was hanged on the wall of his own castle in retaliation for the Protestant who burned at the stake. This sort of thing happened all over Europe during the Protestant Reformation.

"Largely as a result of the Wars of Reformation, much of Europe's population, even now, has abandoned religious practice. Huge cathedrals and churches sit nearly empty, even though a large percentage of the population still iden-tify as Christians."

"Gee, Boss, that's a great story," Jonathan said. "And today we have Muslims killing Christians and Jews in the name of religion. You must be very proud of all you have been able to accomplish, Boss," Jonathan gushed.

"Well, yes. But it wasn't as easy as it sounds. The Koran clearly condemns the killing of innocent people. So I had to overcome that and convince some religious leaders to not only condone murder but to tell their followers that they would be rewarded with virgins in heaven if they killed in-nocent people who follow the God of Abraham, as they do."

"How do you convince people of things like that, Boss?" Jonathan asked.

"Well, the best way to lead religious leaders astray is to start with language from their holy book. There are al-ways ambiguities and room for interpretation," the Boss explained.

"The next key ingredient is the lust for power. While not all religious leaders have that, the most aggressive ones usually do. The ultimate power is a worldwide government based on a religious book led by the supreme religious leader and his key subordinates. You combine that with the old 'ends justify the means' argument, and you have people killing innocent people in order to impose their religion on them.

"This, in turn, results in those under attack defending themselves and killing their attackers. Atrocity leads to atrocity. As attacks become more widespread, homes and businesses are destroyed. Homelessness, disease, and starvation grow widespread. That is exactly what is happening right now in parts of the Middle East.

"It really is great. The amount of human suffering is enormous, and many people commit murder and robbery in these circumstances, and we have an enormous harvest of souls. The truth is, religious wars are my favorite kind of wars," the Boss chortled.

"And in the end, the result is a loss of faith in all religions for many of those who live through a religious war," the Boss instructed.

Chapter 12

)) Eliminating Religion from Public Life

"That all makes sense to me, Boss," Jonathan said. "But there is something I don't understand. At the Academy we were told that eliminating religion from public life in the United States is one of your top priorities right now."

"That's true," the Boss replied.

"Well, but if that is successful, and I know that you will be," Jonathan added, "won't that reduce religious conflict and make it harder to create more religious wars?" Jonathan asked.

"That's an excellent question, Jonathan," the Boss said. "I guess I will need to speak to the headmaster at the Academy to include an explanation of that apparent contradiction in the curriculum," the Boss said.

"The answer is that there are two different tools that can be used to achieve similar results for us," the Boss explained.

"We just discussed religious wars, so I will not repeat

myself about that. Remember our earlier discussion about the breakdown of civil society in the absence of moral values? If the only restraint on murder, theft, assault, and so on is fear of being caught, then, as soon as circumstances suggest that a person will probably not be caught, there will be a large increase in these activities.

"So in order to prepare a whole society for collapse, we must largely eliminate religion. Or, to put it another way, we need to have people believe that there is no God and that there is no inherent right or wrong.

"Eliminating religious belief, or at least substantially reducing the number of people who have religious faith, is something that must be accomplished in a series of steps.

"The first step is to make references to religion in government and in schools unacceptable conduct. We have made considerable progress on that the last hundred years in the United States. And it hasn't been easy.

"For example, here is part of President George Washington's first Thanksgiving proclamation in 1789:

Whereas it is the duty of all Nations to acknowledge the providence of Almighty God, to obey his will, to be grateful for his benefits, and humbly to implore his protection and favor—and whereas both Houses of Congress have by their joint Committee requested me 'to recommend to the People of the United States a day of public thanksgiving and prayer to be observed by acknowledging with grateful hearts the many signal favors of Almighty God especially by affording

them an opportunity peaceably to establish a form of
government for their safety and happiness.'

Now therefore I do recommend and assign Thursday
the 26th day of November next to be devoted by the
People of these States to the service of that great and
glorious Being, who is the beneficent Author of all the
good that was, that is, or that will be—That we may
then all unite in rendering unto him our sincere and
humble thanks—for his kind care and protection of
the People of this Country previous to their becoming a Nation—for the signal and manifold mercies,
and the favorable interpositions of his Providence
which we experienced in the course and conclusion
of the late war—for the great degree of tranquillity,
union, and plenty, which we have since enjoyed.

"There's more. It's all disgusting. But you get the idea.

"And in many public schools in the 1800s students were
required to study the Bible extensively.

"Yes, the early days of the United States were a tough
time for us. The federal Northwest Ordinance set aside land
to endow schools to teach religion and morality. The federal
government paid for missionaries to the Indians—that is,
the Native Americans, as we 'politically correctly' say today. And as late as the end of the 1800s the federal government was financing the construction of religiously affiliated
hospitals.

"Back in those days the people's understanding of the
First Amendment to the United States Constitution was
that the government could give special aid to religion as

long as there was no discrimination between religious sects. The idea was that the government could support religion so long as no single church was officially established and the government did not deny any citizen the right to the free exercise of his or her religion.

"One of the things that really bothered me was that prayers and Bible readings were common in public schools until the early 1960s.

"It wasn't until the 1940s, '50s, and '60s in the United States when I came up with the idea of using the courts to eliminate religion from the public square. Once I put that idea in a few heads, things really took off.

"But it wasn't easy. For a century and a half, the US Supreme Court in its decisions regarded religion favorably.

"For example, in 1844 in the case of *Vidal v. Girard's Executors*, the US Supreme Court said with approval: 'It is also said, and truly, that the Christian religion is a part of the common law of Pennsylvania.'

"And then in 1892 there was a US Supreme Court case, *Holy Trinity Church*, which really discouraged me. The Court said: 'No purpose of action against religion can be imputed to any legislation, state or national, because this is a religious people. This is historically true.'

"And if that wasn't bad enough, the Court went on to give numerous examples. It quoted from the first charter of Virginia granted by King James I in 1606—'By the Providence of Almighty God, hereafter tend to the Glory of his Divine Majesty, in propagating of Christian Religion.'

"Then the Court noted that the charter of privileges

granted by William Penn to the province of Pennsylvania in 1701 contained these words: 'And Almighty God being the only Lord of Conscience, Father of Lights and Spirits; and the Author as well as Object of all divine Knowledge, Faith, And Worship.'

"And to make matters worse, the Court noted the 1780 Constitution of Massachusetts that stated: 'It is the right as well as the duty of all men in public society, and at stated seasons, to worship the Supreme Being, the great Creator and Preserver of the universe.'

"The Court gave many other examples in that case, but the very worst of all was the 1776 Constitution of Delaware, which required all officers to make the following declaration: 'I do profess faith in God the Father, and in Jesus Christ his only Son, and in the Holy Ghost, one God, blessed for evermore; and I do acknowledge the Holy Scriptures of the Old and New Testament to be given by divine inspiration.'

"Can you believe that?" the Boss exclaimed with anger rising in his voice. "So you can see what I was up against!

"But, Jonathan, because I didn't give up, the US Supreme Court has done a great job of reigning in religion beginning in 1947. That year, the Supreme Court ruled that the establishment of religion clause in the United States Constitution was intended to erect 'a wall of separation between church and state.' I could not have been more pleased. That got the ball rolling on pretty much chasing any reference to religion out of the public schools.

"It wasn't until 1962 that the US Supreme Court finally held that school prayer was unconstitutional because it violated the establishment of religion clause of the US Constitution.

"Then in 1990, the Supreme Court, in the *Department of Employment Division* case, ruled that neutral laws of general applicability affecting religious practices do not require religious exemptions.

"While it sounds obscure, that was huge for us! It means that there is no constitutional protection for religious belief in most cases, even though the Constitution says that, 'Congress shall pass no law respecting an establishment of religion, or prohibiting the free exercise thereof.'

For example, people whose religious belief does not recognize same-sex marriage can be compelled by law to participate in the marriage by making cakes or providing photographs and so forth. Religious hospitals can be required to perform abortions contrary to their religious beliefs. What a breakthrough!

"By the way, in your legal studies class, did the instructor explain why that decision was so difficult to achieve?" the Boss asked.

"Yes, sir," Jonathan eagerly replied. "The Supreme Court has held that when a fundamental right is involved, a law will be subject to what the courts call 'strict scrutiny.' That means the government has to show a compelling government interest and achieve its goal by using the least restrictive means available. So the Supreme Court is essentially saying that religious belief is *not* a fundamental right, but burning the American flag, abortion, and same-sex marriage *are* fundamental rights."

"Very good, Jonathan," the Boss commended. "Your legal education has been outstanding!"

"Boss?"

"Yes, Jonathan."

"Do you think that the Supreme Court will ever reverse itself and declare that freedom of religion, that is, the free exercise of religion, is a fundamental right, since it is the first right listed in the First Amendment to the Constitution of the United States?"

"I certainly hope not, but I do have some concern," the Boss confided. "Take, for example, the case of a baker who won't make a wedding cake for a same-sex marriage because of his religious beliefs. Right now, that is not protected as a free exercise of religion by the US Supreme Court. The baker has to argue that it violates his right of free speech because it forces him to use his artistic talents to effectively 'speak' in support of a same-sex union. Even that argument has not yet been endorsed by the United States Supreme Court. And even if it was, it would not protect a Catholic hospital that refuses to perform abortions.

"But the makeup of the United States Supreme Court is changing, so the court may overrule its previous case and hold that free exercise of religion is a fundamental right. That is a realistic possibility and one that worries me, because historically the free exercise clause was understood to protect rights of conscience based on religious belief. In other words, the government could not compel a person to act contrary to his or her religious beliefs. If that were to happen, it would be a big setback for us.

"Another thing that concerns me relates to the *Employment Division* case, which we talked about before. In that case, the Supreme Court, said, in essence, that a neutral law of general applicability is a higher law than the constitutional right to free exercise of religion. This is contrary to the nearly universal rule that a provision of the United States Constitution is a higher law than a statute and that any statute that violates the Constitution is therefore unconstitutional.

"So I am afraid that someday a do-gooder lawyer will convince the Supreme Court that it made a grave error, and the court will once again place the Constitution above a law that favors us.

"But I am encouraged by the fact that the Court, in the case of the baker, could have overturned its previous case and held that the free exercise of religion is a fundamental right but did not do so. So, hopefully, our argument, which is that religious zealots are using their religious belief as an excuse to discriminate against persons wanting abortions or same-sex wedding cakes, will prevail.

"One more thing, Jonathan," the Boss said. "Were you taught at the Academy that another problem we had in eliminating religion from the public square was that so many of the early colleges, in what is now the United States, were founded by religious orders? And they even required religious studies as a central part of their curriculum!" the Boss exclaimed.

"Yes, sir. But I could hardly believe it," Jonathan replied.

"Yes, it is hard for people to believe it now—because of

our success—but early colleges like Harvard, Yale, and others were hard-core religious institutions. For example, look at this from the early days of Harvard College:

> Laws and Statutes for Students of Harvard College
> Harvard College Lawes of 1642
> (from New England's First Fruits)
>
> 2. Every one shall consider the mayne End of his life and studyes, to know God and Jesus Christ which is Eternall life. Joh. 17.3.
>
> 3. Seeing the Lord giveth wisdome, every one shall seriously by prayer in secret, seeke wisdome of him. prov. 2.2,3 etc.
>
> 4. Every one shall so exercise himselfe in reading the Scriptures twice a day that they bee ready to give an account of their proficiency therein...
>
> 6. they shall eschew all prophanation of Gods holy name, attributes, word, ordinances, and times of worship, and study with Reverence and love carefully to reteine God and his truth in their minds.

"It goes on, but you get the idea," the Boss said. "And Yale University was established by clergy to educate Congregational ministers, if you can believe that!

"In fact, the 1787 Yale student guidelines stated: 'All the scholars are required to live a religious and blameless life according to the rules of God's Word, diligently reading the Holy Scriptures, that fountain of Divine light and truth, and constantly attending all the duties of religion.'"

"How were you able to change religious schools like that to what they are today?" Jonathan asked.

"Well, it took time. Some of how we did it is explained in that guy Buckley's book—*God and Man at Yale*. Didn't you study that at the Academy?" the Boss asked.

"Er, well, yes, sir. I guess we did. Maybe I should reread it," Jonathan stammered.

"Yes, you should. Basically, it was like this. Buckley criticized Yale for forcing a secularist ideology on students and argued that several professors tried to break down students' religious beliefs through their hostility to religion. He was correct. That is essentially how I did it.

"But it was in the 1960s and '70s when things really took off. I encouraged colleges to change their policies to allow young unmarried men and women to live together in the same college dormitory. Use the same restrooms. Lots of alcohol and drugs easily available because of lax enforcement. A hookup culture. It's really great!

"And, of course, this results in a lot of premarital sex and unwanted pregnancies. Not to mention, it creates a climate for, and an easy opportunity for, rape. As a result, any number of young men do take advantage of, and force themselves on, young women—particularly on young women who have overconsumed alcohol or are high on drugs.

"But the best part is, the same people who implemented those 'enlightened' policies now demand that colleges crack down on sexual assault and unwanted sexual advances on college campuses! Can you believe it? Am I good or what!" chortled the Boss.

"But does that mean that colleges will eliminate coed dorms and restrooms and start telling kids to wait for sex until they are married?" Jonathan asked.

"No. At least it's very unlikely. To do that, college administrators would have to admit that they were wrong. They think they are too smart to have made a mistake and too proud to admit it in any event.

"So, on the one hand, they will leave in place a system that leaves young women unnecessarily exposed to situations where rape is likely to occur and will occur.

"And, on the other hand, some innocent young men will be denied due process, and their lives will be destroyed either by false accusations by women who gladly consented to sex but now, for whatever reason, have been rejected and want revenge. For example, if the guy starts dating another girl, his prior sexual partner may want revenge. Sometimes human nature makes my job so easy!" the Boss exclaimed.

"As you know, Jonathan, these false accusations are already happening on many college campuses. Remember, for example, the three Duke lacrosse players who were falsely accused of rape by a stripper?

"The generally accepted theory on most college campuses these days is that men can't be trusted and that women never lie about sex. So, in addition to a lot of rapes that college administrators could have prevented with better rules, we can also look forward to some young men having their promising futures destroyed by the very institutions that encourage sex on the one hand and punish those who do it on the other."

"Gee, Boss, that's exactly how you operate, too," Jonathan marveled. "You tempt people with something they desire, and when they do it, they either get hurt or you get their soul, or both," Jonathan said.

"Yes, it is a tried-and-true formula. It worked in the Garden of Eden, and it still works today. And it's great having college administrators helping me lead young men and women into temptation," the Boss smiled.

"So do you control all those college administrators?" Jonathan asked.

"No. Not in the way that you mean. I don't compel them to do it. They decide what they are going to do. We just use our usual tools of desire for power, desire for money, desire for approval by their peers, and desire for recognition. These are very powerful tools.

"Is there a college president of a public university in the United States today who will prohibit coed dorms, prohibit coed restrooms, lecture students not to have premarital sex, or require, or even recommend, that students dress modestly or not drink alcohol?" Jonathan asked.

"Of course not," the Boss replied, "That would not be progressive. That would be trying to impose their values on the students—assuming that they even have those values," he said laughing.

Chapter 13

))Hate

"Did they teach you at the Academy that we now refer to Christianity as a religion of hate?"

"Yes, sir," Jonathan replied to the Boss. "We studied that in our current events class."

"Yes, it is a new approach for us. To be honest, I had my doubts at first about whether it would work. You know with all the Son's preaching about 'Love one another,'[8] 'Turn... the other cheek,'[9] 'Pray for those who persecute you'[10] and all that, I thought it would be a tough sell. But as you know, I can be very persuasive.

"Even so, convincing people that a religion that focuses on love and forgiveness is a religion of hate was a real challenge."

"Yes, Boss, we studied your methods on this at the Academy."

"Good. What were you taught?"

"Basically, that we should make the case that people who

believe in OWNWDNS and try to follow his rules hate people who don't follow the rules," Jonathan replied. "So, for example, we say that the Son's people believe that divorce is wrong, because the Son said so, and that they therefore hate people who get divorced. Or that Christians hate homosexuals because of the rule that 'a man shall not lie with another man as with a woman.'"

"Excellent, Jonathan! I couldn't have said it better myself."

"Thank you, sir. Sir, I have a question."

"What is it?"

"Well, I am glad, of course, that those arguments work so well for us. But the Son will forgive all of the divorcees, the women who get abortions, and the homosexuals who ask for forgiveness. And the Son's followers are also supposed to forgive them and love them. So why does our argument that Christians are haters work so well?"

"Excellent question, Jonathan, although you should've been taught the answer to that at the Academy.

"First of all, some of the Son's followers don't practice what he preached. They don't forgive or love these people. That makes it pretty easy to convince people that Christians are haters.

"In other cases, quite a few of the people getting divorces or aborting their babies or whatever prefer to think that there is nothing wrong with what they do. So they hate the Son's followers because the Son's followers believe these things are wrong. And they assume that the Son's followers hate them in return. We just encourage that assumption.

"It all goes back to a principle that we talked about

earlier—many people prefer to be their own god, deciding for themselves what is right and what is wrong. Or, as many in the intellectual class say, what is right and what is wrong is a social construct. There is no inherent right or wrong. We, of course, strongly encourage this type of thinking.

"Anyway, all of this is really great for us. Many of the Son's followers don't want to be seen as or be called haters, so they withdraw from the public discussion of these issues. Which brings me to one of my favorite sayings by Edmund Burke, 'The only thing necessary for the triumph of evil is for good men to do nothing.'"

"Sir, is the Equality Act that recently passed the US House of Representatives a result of our 'Christians are haters' campaign?"

"Very insightful, Jonathan. It is indeed. That legislation basically says the rights of homosexuals take legal priority over the beliefs of the Son's followers. I just love it when the law is on our side!" the Boss chortled.

Chapter 14

)) Clergy Who Don't Follow the Bible

"One of my recent achievements has been the installation of clergy who don't follow the Bible in their sermons. Some of them don't even believe in the Son, if you can believe that, Jonathan," the Boss bragged.

"Yes, sir," replied Jonathan. "In religion class at the Academy we were taught that undermining the church from within is one of our best tools."

"Correct. So now we have some men and women preachers in Christian churches who won't preach, or in some cases even believe, that there is only one way to get to heaven. This is great for us. What it says is, even people who believe there is a God in heaven don't have to believe in the Son to get there. In fact, for them, the Son is unnecessary— as I have been saying for more than two millennia, I might add."

"Yes, Boss. At the Academy we were encouraged to

promote the idea to the clergy that the Bible should not be taken literally. For example, the world was not really created in six days, there was never a real Adam and Eve, and the Son did not physically come back to life. Boss?"

"Yes, Jonathan."

"How do you convince the clergy of things like that?"

"Great question, Jonathan. There is no one answer. Some of them like *some* of the Son's preaching—like 'Love one another.'[11] And they genuinely want to help people get along with each other. But they don't really believe that a dead person could come back to life, for example. They go into the ministry to help people, but they don't believe the Bible is literally true.

"Others believe the Son was a great teacher whose ideas they want to promote but don't believe he is literally a deity."

"Yes, we were taught at the Academy to promote this idea," Jonathan replied. We were also warned about how C. S. Lewis responded to this argument. He said:

I am trying to prevent anyone saying the really foolish thing that people often say about Him: 'I'm ready to accept Jesus as a great moral teacher, but I don't accept his claim to be God.' That is the one thing we must not say. A man who was merely a man and said the sort of things Jesus said would not be a great moral teacher. He would either be a lunatic—on the level with the man who says he is a poached egg—or else he would be the Devil of Hell. You must make your choice. Either this man was, and is, the Son of God, or else a madman or something worse. You can shut him up for a fool, you can spit at him and kill him as a demon or you can fall at his feet and call him Lord and God, but let us not come with any patronizing nonsense about his being a great human teacher. He has not left that open to us. He did not intend to. Now it seems to me obvious that he was neither a lunatic nor a fiend: and consequently, however strange or terrifying or unlikely it may seem, I have to accept the view that He was and is God.

"Yes," the Boss replied. "But fortunately, not many people know who Lewis is or what he wrote. And in any event, we can always argue that the Son was just a mythical figure anyway.

"Other preachers like the idea of being God themselves. They don't think of it in those terms, of course. They think they have a better understanding of religion than what is in the Bible. To them, the Bible has some good points but should not be taken literally. This means they can decide for themselves what OWNWDNS is like and preach their own ideas as the word of OWNWDNS.

"We encourage all of these approaches by the clergy, of course. But what is even better are the atheists—especially the atheists who go to court to try and make atheism the public religion, so to speak," the Boss said with a smile.

"Yes, sir," Jonathan replied. "We spent a lot of time on atheism in religion class at the Academy."

"What exactly were you taught?"

"The basic concept is that there is no God, no devil, no soul, and no afterlife. Primitive, superstitious human beings invented the idea of God. The Bible is just a fictional story book. The Son, if he ever existed at all, was not a deity but an influential rabbi."

"Yes," the Boss replied, "and, of course, our tools of logic and ridicule are tailor-made for atheism. For example, everyone knows that the earth is millions of years old, not six thousand or seven thousand as the Bible literalists claim. And there is no way a dead person can come back to life. And there is no way a flood could cover the whole earth. No intelligent person could believe those sorts of things. That's our story, and I'm sticking to it," the Boss said with a laugh.

Chapter 15

)) Evil Is Good

"As I mentioned earlier, under the Son's completely unfair rules, all people have to do to defeat us is believe in Him and ask for forgiveness. So one of our most important tactics is to convince people that what they are doing is not wrong. If they believe what they are doing is not wrong, they will not ask for forgiveness, and we win," the Boss reminded Jonathan.

"Yes, they emphasized that at the Academy in our ethics class, sir. They taught us that we should take every opportunity to convince people that good is evil and evil is good," Jonathan said.

"Well said, Jonathan. The courts in the United States, especially the Supreme Court, have been very helpful to us in that regard in recent years," the Boss said with a smile.

"Yes, sir. We spent a lot of time on that in our legal studies class. We were taught that *Roe v. Wade* is a very important case. It basically said a woman has a constitutional right to kill her unborn child. And over sixty million children have been killed so far as a result," Jonathan noted.

"Yes, that was a good case for us. But one of my favorite quotes comes from a later abortion case—*Planned Parenthood of Southeastern Pennsylvania v. Casey.* The court said, 'At the heart of liberty is the right to define one's own concept of existence, of meaning, of the universe, and of the mystery of human life. Beliefs about these matters could not define the attributes of personhood were they formed under compulsion of the State.'

"In other words, to revise a quotation from the Holy Book, everyone should be able to do what is right in their own eyes.[12] I have been telling people that for millennia— and it works very well."

"Why is that, Boss?" Jonathan asked.

"Because most people like the idea of being their own God—deciding for themselves what is good and what is evil.

"That is an important key in getting people to call good evil and evil good. So, for example, calling abortion good when in fact it is evil.

"As I like to say, abortion is good because it lets men and women enjoy sex without the responsibility of having a child. An unwanted child is a financial and emotional burden that can easily be solved by an abortion. And, as a former United States president once said about his daughters, 'I don't want them punished with a baby'. I couldn't have said it better myself," the Boss said with a laugh.

"And there are a lot of other recent decisions from the

United States Supreme Court that are giving people the assurance that various evil things are really good.

"Having already approved of sodomy and ordered states to approve of same-sex marriage, we are on the legal road to even greater things.

"As Justice Scalia pointed out in *Planned Parenthood of Southeastern Pennsylvania v. Casey*, the same legal arguments that support abortion also support polygamy, adult incest, and suicide. Mark my words, Jonathan. It won't be long now before the courts rule that those are constitutional rights as well. How could they not—it's only logical, as I like to say!

"So I hope to see the US courts soon declare a constitutional right to assisted suicide. After all, what is more clearly related to 'the right to define one's own concept of existence' than assisted suicide," the Boss pointed out.

"Yes, we studied that in our advanced legal studies class at the Academy," Jonathan added.

"And can you explain why assisted suicide is an important goal for us?" the Boss asked.

"Yes, sir. Once assisted suicide is accepted as being a good thing, it will expand rapidly."

"And why is that?" the Boss asked.

"Because old people will feel pressured to avoid the pain and expense of a long illness. In some cases, relatives will want to get their hands on the old person's money. And it will also be a way for the US government to reduce Medicare expenses," Jonathan answered as he had been taught in his ethics class.

Chapter 16

)) Don't Make People Uncomfortable

"You will recall our earlier discussion about preachers not doing fire-and-brimstone speeches about the devil and the assignment I gave you on that?" the Boss asked.

"Yes, sir."

"Well, another related project of ours is discouraging preachers from warning people about adultery, divorce, abortion, jealousy, and so forth. If people believe that there is nothing wrong with these things, they won't ask for forgiveness, and we win," the Boss boasted.

"Our most effective tool on this project is compassion, together with a concern by clergy that talking about these subjects will cause people to stop coming to their church.

"The compassion argument is simple," the Boss continued. "Many people who are involved in divorce, abortion, and so forth are already having a difficult time and so, we say, don't make them feel even worse by telling them that these things are wrong in the eyes of OWNWDNS."

"Now I see the connection, Boss. The fire-and-brimstone preachers give sermons about these things and then encourage people to seek forgiveness from the Son."

"Exactly right, Jonathan. Our goal is preachers who see no evil, hear no evil, and especially do not speak about evil. We want people to feel comfortable that there's nothing wrong with the things they are doing."

"At the Academy we studied the recent success you have been having with priests sexually abusing children," Jonathan added.

"Yes, the basic use of one of our better tools—sexual desire. Did they explain at the Academy why this is such an important project?"

"Yes, sir. Because it causes large numbers of people to turn away from organized religion and for many of them to lose faith in OWNWDNS."

"Yes. And we got a bonus recently with the pope dragging his feet on throwing the perverts out of the church and turning them over to law enforcement. When the head of the Catholic Church seems not to care, it weakens the faith of many and causes many others to reject the church entirely."

"How did you manage that, Boss?"

"Just got lucky on that one. It's fascinating really, this pope seems to care more about climate change than about dealing with priests who are helping us undermine his church."

"Yes, but none of it would have happened without all your hard work, Boss."

"Why, thank you, Jonathan," the Boss beamed.

Chapter 17

)) Evolution

"Jonathan, you will recall that some time ago we talked about how we use the concept of evolution to disprove that the earth and everything on it was created in six days."

"Yes, Boss."

"Well, I am concerned that someday some scientist is going to turn it around on us."

"What do you mean, Boss?"

"Well, they know the second law of thermodynamics is that in the absence of an external force or energy, a system becomes more disorganized with the passage of time."

"What does that have to do with evolution, Boss?"

"Consider this. Assume, for the sake of argument, that all life on earth was created in a few days. And also assume that it was all designed perfectly for the then existing climate conditions, but was preprogrammed to adapt to future changes in climate.

"Then, as time went on, and each type of plant and

animal reproduced itself, genetic changes happened from time to time. In other words, they 'evolved' by becoming less perfect than the original plant or animal. Like in thermodynamics, biological systems became more disorganized with the passage of time.

"That would explain the missing links. That is, there are no transitional fossils of one type of animal transitioning to another type of animal because that never happened."

"But, Boss. What about the 'survival of the fittest'? Wouldn't the original creation always be the fittest and so it would survive and the genetic mutations would die off?"

"That would be true if the climate didn't change, rainfall patterns never changed, the temperature of the earth never changed, et cetera. So even though genetic mutations are not perfect copies of the original, they are sometimes better suited to the changes that occur on the earth from time to time. What if scientists start seeing that as part of a plan, instead of random chance?

"Let me explain it another way.

"Scientists now know that many plants and animals have genes that don't seem to have a purpose. Some theorize that they had a purpose earlier but are no longer needed by the organism.

"But what if they start thinking that it is the other way around?"

"What do you mean, Boss?" Jonathan asked.

"Well, what if those genes were created and designed by OWNWDNS for the future. So that a plant or animal could rapidly adapt to a change in conditions—drought, heat, cold, new diseases, et cetera. And that the new conditions switch on those genes so that the organism can rapidly adapt to the new conditions. Let's face it, Jonathan, if it took even a thousand years for a type of plant or animal to adapt to a life-threatening change of conditions, it would die off before it could adapt.

"It's already known," the Boss continued, "that bacteria can adapt very quickly to defeat new medicines designed to kill them. And some insects adapt rapidly to survive poisons designed to kill them."

"Okay, Boss. But I really don't see why all that matters," Jonathan remarked.

"You don't understand why it matters? And you are at the top of your class at the Academy! I guess I will need to have a talk with some of your professors," the Boss said disgustedly.

"It's the difference between random chance and intelligent design," he continued. "In random chance there is no OWNWDNS. In intelligent design, there would be a creator of unimaginable intelligence. Genes designed for future adaption strongly suggests a creator. That kind of thinking makes our job a lot more difficult," the Boss explained.

"But, Boss, don't we still have the argument that science proves that fossils are much older than the creation scientists say?"

"Yes, fortunately. But, of course, that depends on the accuracy of the methods of estimating the age of fossils."

"You mean they are not accurate?" Jonathan asked with astonishment.

"Well, I don't want to get too technical, but carbon dating is based on the assumption that the ratio of carbon-14 to carbon-12 has remained constant—but has it? Carbon-14 is created at a steady rate by radiation from the sun interacting with nitrogen in the atmosphere. But much of the carbon-12 that was once in the atmosphere has been locked away in coal, oil, and methane. So the critical assumption is, shall we say, questionable.

"And not only that. Another method for measuring how old things are is based on radioactive decay rates—that is, the half-life of radioactive elements. That method assumes that radioactive decay rates for various elements are constant. What has been overlooked is that beta decay rates increase dramatically when atoms are stripped of their electrons."

"Wow! This is way beyond anything we studied in science class at the Academy," Jonathan interjected.

"Well, I am extremely knowledgeable about this field," the Boss replied. "Let me continue.

"In 1999, German scientist Dr. Fritz Bosch demonstrated that stripping all of the electrons from a rhenium atom decreased its half-life from forty-two billion years to thirty-three years. Some scientists theorize that the great flood unleashed strong electromagnetic effects that did strip electrons from radioactive elements. The result would be that the earth's age, as measured by radioactive element half-lives, is only thousands of years old."

"Gosh, Boss, how do we handle those problems?"

"The usual way—ridicule and logic. We can say that the

people making those arguments are pseudoscientists who are really religious fanatics and that most scientists don't agree with them. Hopefully, that will continue to work," the Boss said with a hint of concern in his voice.

"But I just wish we didn't have to deal with these sorts of things. Our job is tough enough as it is, with the Son going around forgiving people."

"I know, Boss. But consider how successful you have been. We have way more souls here with us than OWNWDNS has," Jonathan pointed out.

"Well, that's true," the Boss agreed. "And if we want to keep that record going, we need to get back to work."

Chapter 18

)) A Pregnant Girlfriend

"I have an assignment for you, Jonathan," the Boss said.

"Yes, sir. What is it?"

"A young man, Jim Andrews, has recently learned that his girlfriend is pregnant with his child. He is seriously considering marrying her. I want you to convince him not to marry her and instead pressure her to have an abortion. As you know, this is usually very simple, so I expect a good result."

"Yes, sir. I will get right on it."

Jonathan began by doing some research on Jim Andrews. He was twenty years old and was a junior at a state university. He had excellent grades and intended to go on to medical school. His parents were experiencing some financial problems, so Jim was using student loans to finance his education.

His girlfriend, Anna Jensen, was a waitress at a restaurant near campus where Andrews sometimes went to eat. They had been dating for about a year, and they had recently talked about perhaps getting married after Andrews finished his undergraduate education.

Andrews, together with three of his friends, was renting a house near campus. By splitting the rent four ways, it was cheaper for them to live there than in a college dormitory.

One of the friends had recently decided that college was not really for him and was leaving to join a high-tech start-up company. So Andrews and his friends were looking for a new roommate.

One evening, Jonathan knocked on the door to their house. Jim Andrews answered the door.

"Hello, I'm Jonathan," Jonathan said. "I heard on campus that you are looking for a new roommate to share expenses."

"Yes, we are," Jim replied. "Please come in.

"Can you tell me a little about yourself?" Jim asked.

"Of course," Jonathan replied.

"I recently transferred from a community college and have been looking for a place to live here that isn't too expensive. When I heard that you and your friends were looking for a new roommate, it sounded like just what I was looking for."

"What are you studying, Jonathan?"

"Prelaw. I seem to have a knack for making logical arguments, so it seems like a good fit," Jonathan replied.

"I see," Jim replied. "Well, one fourth of the rent is $400 a month. Does that work for you?"

"That would be perfect," Jonathan replied.

"There's one more thing that I should tell you before you join us," Jim said.

"What's that?" Jonathan asked.

"Well, I may be leaving in the near future to get married, so you may soon be searching for another new roommate."

"Well, congratulations," Jonathan replied. "I was recently dating a girl who wanted to marry me. But after thinking about it, I decided I wasn't really ready to get married. I can barely afford the expense of college as it is, let alone law school. I was afraid that if we got married, I would have to drop out of school and give up my dreams of being a lawyer. It was a bad situation. She was pregnant and everything."

"Wow, that sounds a lot like my situation," Jim replied. "I like her a lot, and she wants to get married and raise our child together. But we can't live on what she makes as a waitress, especially after the baby comes. And I already have a ton of student loans. I think I could work part time and finish college, but there is no way I could go to medical school if we get married and she has a baby."

"I'm really sorry to hear that," Jonathan replied. "But you plan to marry her anyway?"

"Well, I really feel like I should."

"Why? This wouldn't have happened if she had used birth control."

"Well, that's true."

"And you could ask her to get an abortion—problem solved," Jonathan suggested.

"We did talk about that, but she is strongly against it."

"Let me see if I understand this," Jonathan said. "You have to give up your dream of being a doctor because she won't get an abortion. Is that right?"

"Well, yes."

"That doesn't seem fair to me. Why don't you tell her that you will marry her if she gets an abortion first?"

"I don't think she will go for that," Jim replied.

"Well, if it was me, I would tell her that if she would not do that for me, then she doesn't really love me and we shouldn't get married. But it's your life, Jim."

"Maybe you have a point," Jim said. "I think that I will have another talk with her."

"Angelica, I have another assignment for you."

"Yes, Sir," Angelica replied.

"Anna Jensen has just been told by her boyfriend, Jim Andrews, that unless she gets an abortion, he will not marry her and will leave her. I want you to convince her to give birth to her baby."

"Yes, Sir."

Angelica knew that the odds were against her, but she was determined to do her best.

Angelica saw Anna sitting by herself on a park bench crying.

"Hello," Angelica said gently. "I couldn't help but notice that you have been crying. What can I do to help?"

At the sound of Angelica's voice Anna looked up. She saw bright light that seemed to shine on Angelica, but it quickly faded.

"I don't see what anyone can do to help," Anna sniffled. "My boyfriend basically said if I don't get an abortion, he is going to abandon me. I don't know what to do."

"That is so sad," Angelica replied. "I would think that if he really loved you that he would marry you and raise your child together," Angelica said.

"I know! I think so, too, but he said having a baby now would ruin his life, and if I loved him, I would get an abortion. Maybe I should just get an abortion. Maybe that would solve everything," Anna sobbed.

"Anna, please don't kill your baby. I know women who had abortions years ago, and they still cry for the child they lost. For them, the pain never goes away. There's a better way. You could put your baby up for adoption. There are so many families who would love to adopt your baby."

"Do you really think so?" Anna said.

"I know so. Here is a phone number of a Christian adoption agency that will help you with everything, including financial assistance with medical expenses."

"I will think about it, I promise," Anna said.

As Angelica was leaving, she ran into Jonathan.

"Why were you talking to Anna Jensen?" Jonathan asked.

"How do you know her?" Angelica asked.

"I am a friend of her boyfriend. I'm trying to help him with the problem she is causing him. Wait a minute. Aren't you the one who helped Pastor Smith get out of his legal problems?"

"Yes, that was me. Now I know who you are and who

your boss is," Angelica replied. "Don't you feel guilty about all the problems you cause people?"

"Why should I?" Jonathan replied somewhat defensively. "I like to think that I'm actually helping people," he added. "Right now, as I said, I am helping Jim Andrews solve the problem this Jensen woman is causing him."

"Oh, right," Angelica replied sarcastically. "Breaking Anna Jensen's heart, promoting abortion, trying to destroy the life of Pastor Smith. That isn't helpful to anyone except your boss."

"Hey, miss-high-and-mighty! The way I see it, you are trying to destroy Jim Andrew's life by convincing that Jensen woman not to get an abortion."

"You are almost as good at promoting evil as your boss, aren't you?" Angelica said raising her voice.

"I will take that as a compliment," Jonathan replied, while thinking that something about Angelica made him uncomfortable. The truth was, for all his persuasive ability, Jonathan had always felt a bit uncomfortable doing his job. *What's wrong with me?* Jonathan thought to himself.

Angelica, who had extraordinary intuition, sensed that Jonathan was different from all the other evildoers she had encountered.

"I have a suggestion," Angelica said. "You've done your job. Jim Andrews did exactly what you persuaded him to do. You can leave now, go back to your boss, and report your success."

"I suppose I could do that," Jonathan replied. "But then what?"

"Leave the rest to me," Angelica replied.

With Jonathan gone, Angelica approached Jim Andrews as he was leaving his house.

"Are you Jim Andrews?" Angelica asked.

"Yes. And who are you?"

"My name is Angelica. I am a friend of Anna's."

"Look. I don't want to talk about it. Just leave me alone," Jonathan replied angrily.

"Jim, Anna loves you, and I think you love her."

"If she loved me, she would get an abortion," Jim replied.

"She does love you, Jim. That's why she wants to save your baby's life."

"What did you say?"

"I said that Anna wants to save your baby's life because she loves you."

Jim had never thought about it that way before. "But what about my future?" Jim replied.

"If you really don't want your baby, Anna will give it up for adoption. Is that what you want?"

Jim didn't know what to say. It did seem like a good solution. He could go on with his career just as he had planned. But if Anna loved him and their baby that much …

After a long pause, Angelica said, "Jim, I think you should talk to Anna again about your future together."

"Yeah, I guess I will," Jim said.

A few days later Jim went to see Anna. "Hi, Anna."

"Hello Jim," Anna replied.

"Anna, I've been thinking. Do you really want to get married and have our baby?"

"Oh, Jim. Of course, I do. I love you, and just this morning I felt our baby move inside of me. It was strange and exciting all at the same time."

"Really? Well, I have been doing some research. Our state is desperate for doctors in rural parts of the state. So they have a program to help with medical school expenses if I will promise to locate to a small town in this state after I graduate from medical school. Would you be willing to do that with me?"

"Oh, Jim, of course!"

"In that case I have a question I want to ask you. Anna Jensen, will you marry me?"

"Yes! Yes!"

"Jonathan, how could you let that happen?" the Boss thundered.

"I don't know, sir. I had him convinced that marrying his girlfriend and having a baby would ruin his life. I thought it was a done deal."

"Well, I have learned that you had a conversation with someone by the name of Angelica," the Boss replied menacingly.

A feeling of fear enveloped Jonathan. "Yes, sir. But I had already accomplished my mission at that point," Jonathan stammered.

"If you'd stayed on the job, this marriage might have been prevented and the baby might've been aborted. I am concerned about the influence this Angelica seems to have on you."

"Oh! No, sir. Sorry, sir. This won't happen again."

"It had better not," the Boss growled and waved Jonathan out of his presence.

Chapter 19

)) Infanticide

"I see that in the United States they are bringing back one of my old favorites," the Boss said. "Like Solomon said, 'There is nothing new under the sun.'"[13]

"What do you mean, Boss?" Jonathan asked.

"Infanticide, Jonathan. Infanticide. The governor of New York is for it. The governor of Virginia is for it. Some US Senators are for it."

"Oh! Yes, sir. We studied infanticide in our ethics class at the Academy. It's part of the larger classification of human sacrifice. For example, some people used to throw virgins into a volcano to appease the volcano god."

"Yes. But one of my favorites," the Boss continued, "was sacrificing babies to the god Molech. You can read about it in the Bible. And I have the statue right here in my office.

"As you can see, Molech was a large metal statue with his arms held out in front of him and a fire burning underneath the arms. The arms would get very hot, and the parent or religious leader would lay the child on the arms. You should've heard those little babies scream! It was a very painful death," said the Boss with an evil smile.

Even Jonathan, who had been hardened by the teaching at the Academy, had a feeling of revulsion. He was careful not to let his feelings show to the Boss.

"Will they ever be that cruel to their babies in the United States?" Jonathan asked.

"Oh, they already are. The difference is they cannot hear the baby scream because she is still in the womb when she is dismembered piece by piece.

"Now some do-gooder politicians are pushing for laws that would prohibit abortion when the unborn child is able to feel pain or has a heartbeat. Some states in the United States have passed, or soon will pass, laws like that. But I think we can count on the Supreme Court to throw these laws out," the Boss said confidently.

"Well, Boss. You've done amazing work these last several decades. Sixty million innocent children killed, sodomy, and same-sex marriage legally approved. And as a bonus, people who won't help with same-sex marriages like the baker in Colorado and the flower lady in Washington State are punished by law. You have even been successful in getting assisted suicide approved in several places and infanticide endorsed by several political leaders. It's really amazing."

"Well, yes it is, if I do say so myself," the Boss said with a smile.

Chapter 20

))Death and Destruction?

"You know, Jonathan, sometimes I am surprised myself at all of the success," the Boss boasted. The thing about it is though, in the past when I have been successful, OWNWDNS sometimes steps in.

"For example, we were doing very well back when Noah was alive. And what happened? OWNWDNS killed almost everyone in a flood. It wasn't all bad, though; we had a lot of poor souls join us all at once.

"And then, when we had things going in Sodom and Gomorrah, it was the same thing. OWNWDNS killed them all, except Lot and his two daughters.

"And then when they made that golden calf in the desert—one of my most impressive feats—many of my supporters were killed. On the bright side of that, they all joined us here too."

"Is something like that going to happen in the United States, since you have been so successful recently?"

Jonathan asked.

"It's hard to say. I have no control over that, of course. But a long-term collapse of the electrical grid, a major nuclear war, or a new infectious disease for which there is no cure could each kill hundreds of millions of people in almost no time at all. But I don't think OWNWDNS will do it himself like the flood or Sodom and Gomorrah.

"For the last several thousand years his method has simply been to not prevent evil things from happening. For example, when the Jews in Israel and Judah turned to us, OWNWDNS removed his protection, and they were conquered by the Babylonians and others. Thousands were killed. So I could see something along those lines if we continue to be successful.

"OWNWDNS might even give me the all-clear to do it myself," the Boss said.

"Really?" Jonathan asked with some surprise.

"Sure. Didn't you study Job at the Academy?"

"Oh! Yes, sir. Of course."

"Well then, as you know, he let me do quite a number on Job. I took all of Job's wealth and killed all his children. But I couldn't crack him, and OWNWDNS eventually gave him back his wealth and a new family.

"If I got the chance to do what I did to Job today to every person on earth, I think a very large number of people would reject OWNWDNS and be joining us here," the Boss said confidently.

Chapter 21

)) A Personal Question

"Boss, can I ask you a personal question?"

"Of course, Jonathan. What is it?"

"Were you in heaven once?"

"Yes. And it was quite a show when I left. The Son said I fell 'like lightning!'"[14]

"Why did you leave?"

"Well, it's complicated. But I could see that I would never get to run the show if I stayed. And I knew from the beginning that I had a rare talent for convincing people to do what I wanted them to do. And I proved it right out of the blocks—convincing Eve to eat the forbidden fruit. And that was just the beginning!

"And there's another reason I left—nepotism."

"Nepotism? What do you mean, Boss?" Jonathan asked.

"Well, when I was there, I hate to admit it, but at first I tried to be good. To do good things. But it was never enough. OWNWDNS always favored his Son."

"So I could see that I would never get ahead. And, frankly, I was sick of trying to do good. And so I left to set up a competing operation. Relying on people's greed, lust, jealousy, and so forth has made me tremendously successful, if I do say so myself," the Boss boasted.

Chapter 22

)) Their Own God

"You know, Jonathan," the Boss said, "we have mentioned it before but I want to be clear about what you were taught at the Academy about everyone being his or her own God."

"Yes, sir. We were taught that there is a tendency of people to want to be their own God, but most people don't think about it that way," Jonathan replied, as he had been taught at the Academy.

"Go on."

"Yes, sir. People's subconscious desire to be their own God is not something we use directly—Eve was an exception, of course."

"Of course," the Boss replied.

"Instead we encourage the desire to be their own God with language about freedom and choice and wisdom," Jonathan continued.

"Very good. Can you give me some examples?"

"Yes, sir. One is the catchphrase "my body, my choice." It's used most often to justify abortion but can also be applied to things like addictive drugs and suicide. For example, the argument goes, it's my body that I put the drugs into, so I should be free to decide to use whatever I want. It's nobody else's business.

"But it has many other uses as well," Jonathan continued. "Like a young man who gets his girlfriend pregnant and then tells her he is not going to ruin his life by marrying her. It's his life, so it's his choice. He doesn't think of it in terms of being his own God, but that is the underlying principle that we are exploiting."

"Your mention of a pregnant girlfriend reminds me of your failure with the Andrews couple and that Angelica person. You haven't been in contact with her again by any chance, have you?" the Boss asked with some suspicion in his voice.

"Oh, no, sir! You can count on me to steer clear of her," Jonathan assured him.

"Well, I would hope so," the Boss replied.

"Now, where were we? Oh, yes. We were talking about abortion and a person being his or her own God," the Boss continued.

"In the case of an abortion, the woman, sometimes at the urging of her boyfriend, gets to decide what is good and what is evil, and they get to decide whether their unborn baby lives or dies—very powerful stuff," the Boss said with a smile. "What are some other examples of our use of the 'being your own God' principle?"

"Well, sir, we were taught that there are quite a few. One,

of course, is atheism. That is very simple—if there is no God, then you can be your own God and do whatever is right in your own eyes. But, of course, they don't think of it that way. They just think the idea that there is a God is preposterous. Not to mention, they don't like the idea that there are rules they are supposed to follow.

"More subtle examples include some intellectuals who believe there is a God, but that they have a better understanding of what God is, and should be, than what is written in the Bible," Jonathan continued.

"An even more subtle example is the people sometimes referred to as the 'elites.' They believe that the laws apply to the 'little people' but don't apply to them."

"Excellent, Jonathan. And just to emphasize the point one more time—few, if any, of these people understand that the underlying principle we are using is that they can be their own God. No. No. No. As we say, it is about freedom and choice and wisdom," the Boss grinned.

Chapter 23

)) Public Opinion

"While, of course, we work one-on-one to achieve our goals," the Boss said, "one of the best ways to be successful on a large scale is to influence public opinion. More specifically, to convince people that what is good is evil and what is evil is good.

"So, as we discussed previously, abortion is good because it gives women a choice. Divorce is good because it lets people out of an unhappy marriage.

"We also try to get things that are good labeled as evil. For example, we say that someone who believes in traditional marriage is a bigot and a hater. Someone who opposes letting men who say they are women use the women's restroom is homophobic. Someone who supports controlling the southern border of the United States is a racist.

"I just love it when humans throw around these negative labels!" the Boss exclaimed.

"One of my favorite tools is addictive drugs. Like most of our tools, they work so well because at first, they give pleasure. They make the user feel good. But in the end, they destroy people's lives and create suffering while they live, plus we get many of them at the end too," the Boss said with a grin.

"Drug addiction usually leads to a breakdown in the family and can lead to theft, robbery, assault, prostitution, and so forth to get money to feed the addiction. If the addict has children, the children suffer. And when the addict can't get his drugs, he suffers withdrawal symptoms. So once we get someone started on addictive drugs, the rest of our work pretty much takes care of itself."

"Boss, are you concerned that they will make addictive drugs legal?" Jonathan asked. "They say it would lower the cost and so there would be less theft and prostitution and so forth to get money to buy the drugs."

"That's a good question, Jonathan. As a matter fact, I am strongly in support of the idea of legalizing illegal drugs. I have been working with opinion leaders to encourage public support for the idea.

"For this to be successful requires an incremental approach. Marijuana seems to be the best place to begin. The first step is to support medical marijuana. It is easy to generate sympathy for medical marijuana because there are people with serious medical problems who sincerely believe that marijuana, at a minimum, helps relieve their symptoms. And perhaps in some circumstances that is true, although there have been few, if any, scientific studies to support that. In any event, people are sympathetic to those who are suffering and want to help.

"The next step is recreational marijuana. This has already been approved in several states in the United States. Our focus here is to downplay the scientific evidence that heavy marijuana use damages certain parts of the brain—particularly in young people. We also worked to deemphasize the increase in traffic accidents by those using marijuana.

"Has your statistics department verified these accidents?" asked Jonathan.

"Of course they have," scolded the Boss. "Now, where was I? Oh, yes …

"Different drugs work differently. Some make people more aggressive. Making those drugs more readily available will lead to more domestic assaults. Other drugs suppress the central nervous system and make people lethargic. So they will miss work and get into financial trouble.

"But for most of the drugs, as time goes on the user needs more and more of the drug to get the desired effect. This eventually leads to fatal overdoses in many cases. So, if addictive drug use becomes more widespread, there will be many more deaths from drug overdoses.

"Indeed, even though OxyContin and fentanyl are restricted drugs, we are seeing dramatic increases in drug overdose deaths in those two drugs alone. Imagine the possibilities if those two drugs and others like them were widely available without a prescription," the Boss said with a smile.

"Another aspect of influencing public opinion is what is

sometimes called 'political correctness,'" the Boss continued.

"I like political correctness. The people who insist on political correctness are seen as elitist, arrogant, and condescending by those who they call 'irredeemable deplorables.' So political correctness helps breed animosity between people.

"A lot of this political correctness is really just crazy—a word that is now a politically incorrect word. And the term 'politically correct' is now also labeled politically incorrect. You have to love that!" the Boss laughed.

"The list of what is politically correct goes on and on. For example, 'man up'; 'basket case'; 'long time no see'; 'no can do'; and 'grandfathered in'—all of them and so many more are now on the politically incorrect list—if I may use that term," the Boss laughed.

"What we learned at the Academy," Jonathan added, "was that the important thing to us about political correctness is that it stifles public discussion of religion and religious symbols."

"Absolutely correct. Very good, Jonathan. Yes, Merry Christmas is now happy holidays. Christmas cards are holiday cards. Christmas vacation in schools is now a winter holiday. Christmas concerts are now holiday concerts. Wishing someone a Merry Christmas is now frowned on. Easter vacation is now spring break."

"We also learned," Jonathan added, "that a lot of politically incorrect speech is now deemed to be hate speech. So someone is no longer just politically incorrect—he or she is now a hater."

"Yes," the Boss replied. "All of this helps create a feeling among many people that there is something wrong or embarrassing or even hateful about religion—or at least the Son's religion. It helps weaken religious belief and greatly reduces public profession of religious faith.

"Yes, there is a lot to like about political correctness," the Boss said with a tone of satisfaction.

"Right, Boss," Jonathan replied. "At the Academy we learned that political correctness is the application of the power of being offended. For example, 'Don't talk about your religious beliefs because it offends me. Don't say Merry Christmas because I am an atheist, and it offends me. Don't say that God only approves of marriage between a man and a woman because that offends me.'"

"Correct, Jonathan. And the reason that 'being offended' suppresses much public discussion of religion in the United States is because many Christians believe this 'love one another'[15] idea so they don't want to offend people by talking about their religion—so the offended win. That is, religion is largely forced out of the public square by the 'offended,'" the Boss instructed.

"Of course, another very important opportunity to influence public opinion over the long term is the educational system," the Boss continued.

"For example, if schoolchildren are taught in school that the earth is billions of years old and that dinosaurs lived tens of millions of years ago, most of them will not question it when they are older. Better yet, after they become adults, they will think anyone who has a different opinion about these things doesn't know what he or she is talking about.

"More recently, we have had success in some schools with sex education programs teaching that abortion is a good option. Even better, in some schools, if a boy thinks he's a girl, he can use the girls' restroom, and locker room, and compete in athletics on a girls' team. And when parents of real girls object to that, they are called bigoted and homophobic.

"Of course, we have nearly eliminated any reference to religion in public schools. And we have convinced many school administrators that teaching about Western civilization and American history is divisive and smells of white supremacy.

"So we are having great success working with the educational system," the Boss concluded with satisfaction.

Chapter 24

))Creation Science

"You know, Jonathan," the Boss said one day, "one of the things that worries me is the work of some scientists whose studies tend to confirm the creation story and the great flood."

"What you mean, Boss?"

"For example, there are scientific studies that conclude the entire world's human population descended from one man and one woman.

"It all has to do with DNA. Outside the nucleus of every human cell there are thousands of mitochondrial DNA (mtDNA) that come only from the mother, who got it from her mother, et cetera. In 1987, a team at the University of California at Berkeley published a study comparing the mtDNA of one hundred forty-seven people from five different parts of the world. The study concluded that all one hundred forty-seven had the same female ancestor. She is now called the 'mitochondrial Eve.' More recent study by

Stoeckle and Thaler in 2018 also determined that all humans descended from the same man and woman.

"Fortunately, there remains a scientific dispute as to whether this original man and woman lived one hundred thousand to two hundred thousand years ago or about six thousand five hundred years ago. The answer to that depends on how fast mutations in mtDNA occur. In 1997, a scientific study determined that mutations in mtDNA occur twenty times faster than was previously thought. Using the new rate, mitochondrial Eve lived about six thousand five hundred years ago.

"If that wasn't bad enough, there are scientists whose calculations of what the energy output of the sun was four and a half billion years ago show that it wasn't as great as today. If that is true, the earth would've been an ice planet when life was supposed to be developing. It is called the faint sun paradox.

"Gee, I never heard of that at the Academy," Jonathan interrupted.

"Well, I have a team working on the new curriculum as we speak," the Boss responded.

"Anyway, the faint sun paradox is, on the one hand, early earth needed to have liquid water for most life to develop, but the sun's energy output, if it behaved as other stars, was only seventy percent of what it is today—which would mean that early earth had ice rather than liquid water on its surface.

"Creation scientists, as they are sometimes called, use these calculations and problems as proof the earth and sun are much younger than four and a half billion years.

"And other scientific studies are causing problems too," the Boss continued.

"For instance, it is generally accepted that some galaxies are billions of light-years from Earth. That means the universe must be billions of years old or we could not see the light from those galaxies. However, the unstated assumption for that to be true is that the speed of light is the same today as it was in the past.

"But now there are scientists who have observed that more recent measurements of the speed of light show a lower speed of light than measurements made years earlier. M. E. J. Gheury de Bray in 1927 based his conclusion on measurements spanning seventy-five years.

"More recently, Russian cosmologist, V. S. Troitskii, at the Radiophysical Research Institute in Gorky, determined that the speed of light was ten billion times faster when the universe began."

"What are you getting at?" asked Jonathan.

"Well, if that is correct, then the light from the distant galaxies has reached the earth in a few thousand years rather than several billion years. That strongly suggests a much younger universe, which would tend to support the creation story in the Bible."

"But, Boss, didn't Einstein prove that the speed of light is constant?"

"Well, we like to say that. But that is not what Einstein said," the Boss replied. "Einstein just said that the speed of light is independent of the velocity of the light source. He never studied or theorized about whether the speed of light has always remained constant throughout time. I would like to keep that under wraps, though, so don't go spreading it around."

"You bet, Boss; I won't!" Jonathan replied.

"And then there is the flood," continued the Boss. "There is a scientist by the name of Walter Brown who has a PhD in mechanical engineering from MIT and has taught college courses in physics, mathematics, and computer science. He has written an entire scientific book that explains the mechanics of a worldwide flood, where the water came from, how the explosive release of massive amounts of subterranean water raised mountains and created ocean trenches, created oil and coal deposits, and so forth.

"Fortunately for us, the media and many other scientists view the creation scientists as at best mistaken and, more likely, quacks or religious nuts."

"So, what is the problem?" Jonathan asked.

"The problem is someday these creation scientists may be taken seriously. For hundreds of years, earlier scientists believed the sun, moon, and planets all revolved around the earth. They created complex formulas to describe what they called epicycles—that is that the celestial bodies followed repeated patterns. When the concept that the earth revolves around the sun was first presented, it was strongly denounced by the scientists of the day."

"So what can we do to keep creation scientists from being believed, Boss?"

"We must keep using our tools of logic and ridicule. You

know the story line—creating the earth in six days is an impossible fairytale, a worldwide flood is impossible, and people who believe these things are religious nuts. That sort of thing.

"One of the most helpful things to us, as I said before, is the educational system, which teaches that the earth is four and half billion years old, dinosaurs lived tens of millions of years ago, and so forth. Once these things are accepted by most people as fact, as they are today, any scientific evidence to the contrary will be dismissed or ignored. I just love it when scientists who present evidence that dispute those teachings are denounced as incompetent or as religious zealots."

"It sounds to me like you really have that covered, Boss."

"Yes. But I am still concerned. There are some people who ask where all the matter and energy in the universe came from in the first place. There is no scientific explanation of that even today. And there are those who question how the extremely complex human DNA, the eye, and all the organs that need to work perfectly together could have resulted from random chance. But perhaps I am worrying needlessly. As you said, we have it covered," the Boss said with a certain lack of conviction.

Chapter 25

)) Jonathan and Angelica

"What are you doing here?" Angelica asked Jonathan with a tone of annoyance in her voice.

"I was sent to help Bob Jones and Alice Jones get a divorce," Jonathan responded. "I suppose that you are here to try to keep them together."

"As a matter fact I am. They have three young children, you know," Angelica replied.

"Yes, I know. We hope that with the father no longer in the home some of the children will get into trouble. You know the statistics—eighty-five percent of all youths in prison, seventy-five percent of all adolescent patients in chemical abuse treatment ..."

"Yes, I know the statistics," Angelica said, interrupting him. "How can you be so cruel? Don't you ever feel guilty about all the evil you do?"

"No," Jonathan lied. He had always known he was a little different than the Boss's other assistants. He had excelled at the Academy because of his extraordinary ability to absorb and retain what he was taught there. And working for the Boss could be exciting sometimes. But he often felt uncomfortable doing the Boss's dirty work and about all the pain he was causing.

Angelica sensed some uncertainty in Jonathan's voice. "You know, you don't have to keep doing what you're doing," Angelica said gently.

"Oh yeah? Well maybe you don't need to keep doing what you're doing," Jonathan snapped back.

"Well, actually I do. I am an angel you know," Angelica said quietly.

"Well, aren't you a goody two shoes! Of course I know what you are." In spite of himself, Jonathan couldn't help but like Angelica. *She was so kind and beautiful,* Jonathan thought to himself.

"I really want to help you, Jonathan," Angelica said gently.

"Help me how?"

"I can tell that you are not like the rest of them. I have come into contact with many of your coworkers. They are all evil to the core. They enjoy causing pain, but you are different. I can sense it."

Jonathan didn't know what to say. If the Boss ever found out about this conversation, Jonathan knew he would be in big trouble.

Finally, Jonathan stammered, "What if I am a little different? So what? You know where I come from. I have no choice in the matter. I have nowhere else to go."

"I know that it seems that way, Jonathan. But you do have

a choice. You can come with me. I really like you, Jonathan, and I want to help you."

"Get real, Angelica. Your boss would never let someone like me come with you. Look at all the horrible things that I have done. But, especially, look at where I come from."

"Well, Jonathan, it would be the first time that this has been done, that's for sure. But you've never been anywhere else. Unlike the souls who are now with you and your boss, you never were given the chance to ask the Son for forgiveness. They were given the chance and refused."

"So, are you saying that if I asked the Son for forgiveness for all the evil I have done, I can come with you and never have to go back to the Boss?"

"Yes, Jonathan. Oh, please do," Angelica pleaded with love in her voice.

It seems too good to be true, Jonathan thought to himself. After a long pause he said, "I want to do it, Angelica. Will you help me?"

"Of course. Come with me, Jonathan. I'll take you to the Son myself."

Footnotes

1 Micah 6:8 (RSV)

2 Hebrews 11:1 (RSV)

3 Genesis 15:6 (ISV)

4 Matthew 7:13-14 (RSV)

5 Mark 10:25 (NLV)

6 Author Unknown

7 Exodus 20:13 (KJV)

8 John 13:34 (RSV)

9 Paraphrase of Matthew 5:39 (NIV)

10 Matthew 5:44 (NIV)

11 John 13:34 (RSV)

12 Paraphrase of Deuteronomy 12:8 (RSV)

13 Ecclesiastes 1:9 (NIV)

14 Luke 10:18 (RSV)

15 John 13:34 (RSV)